Hammered

Preston Brothers Book Two

Nicole Falls

Content Warning

*Contains parental illness, high-level discussion of
death*

Acknowledgments

The usuals (C, J, S, S): juuuuuuu already know what it is. Love y'all deep.

Beta boos: Jaleesa, Jilly, Natasha thank you for your time and energy and feedback. You girls are the bees knees

My C-Suite & Mid-level Patreon boos: Chelsea, Christina, Ebony, Honor, Jaleesa, Janielle, Kanika, Krystin, Malaika, Marie, Monica, Moniqua, Natasha B., Natasha P., Raena, Selena—y'all the real MVPs! xo

Wayland

She is entirely too fine to be walking around here with that sour ass look on her face.

As soon as I'd found out that she was going to be involved with the show, I'd known that there was a strong likelihood that the... I hesitated to say beef since it was a one-sided thing as far as I was concerned, but the tension between her and I was bound to come to a boil sooner rather than later.

We'd been filming a new show for CanDo network, Megamansion Makeover, with me and Will, Timi who'd won the first season of the home design show my brother and I had created, Chase who was a carpenter that we worked with often, Ciji Sinclair who was a new rising star on the network, and Kalise who our producer Rachel had brought on to provide all of the plants and flowers for the external makeover of the home.

Kalise who had also been one of my best friends since childhood until I'd fucked things up with that situation.

Kalise who had reappeared after being gone from where we'd grown up for over a decade looking decidedly different from the girl that I'd pledged to be "friends forever" with.

Kalise who, and I'd only ever admitted this to myself, was absolutely my one who got away.

I'd made a bad decision that not only ended up blowing up in my face, but had also lost me the one person, outside of my brother, who had known me the very best. Hell, truthfully, she probably knew me better than my brother because at one time we were just that close. However, we'd spent the last three months working together and you would have thought that we were strangers just based on our interactions. Kalise avoided being alone with me at all costs, denying me the opportunity to really talk to her. Any opportunity that I'd been given to hash things out with her in these past few months, she'd effortlessly dodged and quite frankly I was sick of it.

"Now you're the one looking like somebody stole your bike at a wrap party," my brother Will jibed from beside me. "My how the tables have turned."

"I'm not looking like anything, I'm just...thinking."

"Sure, bro. However you wanna play it. I told you how to resolve this months ago," he spoke up again after a half minute of silence passed between us.

"You think I haven't tried?" I said, turning to him with clear distress on my face.

"I think you haven't tried *hard enough*," he replied. "And since turnabout is fair play, it's only right that I rub it in your face right now."

I shook my head. "Nah man, *that* situation was different. You were trying to shirk your destiny. This ain't that with her."

"Sure, *Tony*."

I shook my head at him using a nickname that had never quite sounded right coming from anyone's lips but the person who'd given it to me. Moving my gaze from my brother to that aforementioned person, I noticed that the mean mug she'd been previously sporting was now a stunningly brilliant smile as she reacted to something that one of the folks who'd joined—and now surrounded her—had said.

Still *so fucking pretty.*

"You gon keep hawking or you coming with me?" my brother asked before he took off to join the group across the room without waiting for my answer.

I wasn't surprised. Hell, there was rarely a moment where he wasn't running up behind Ciji and she was one of the three women and one guy that'd congregated together, whispering and giggling about God knew what. I couldn't front on him though because Ciji Sinclair was a good look for my brother. I loved that dude to death, but he could be a bit uptight and stodgy. In these past few months that he and Ciji had been together though? He was much more relaxed and easygoing. I had no idea what she had done to him to get his attitude to make damn near a one-eighty, but shoutout to her for making everyone's lives around us much easier by getting bro to lighten up.

I walked up to join the group just as a waiter passed by with a tray full of champagne flutes, so I snagged him and diverted his course, making sure everyone in our little circle had a fresh glass before prompting them all to raise their glasses for a toast.

"To Rachel and her big ass brain, for seeing the vision in that dilapidated piece of shit she found for us to turn into what might be one of the best flips I've had the honor of participating in. And to Ciji and Timi for your impeccable eyes for design."

"And Cienna!" TImi chimed in.

"Yeah, where is Ci?" Ciji asked as she frowned.

"Curt whisked her away for some clandestine ass getaway," Rachel chimed in.

"Oh!" Ciji exclaimed. "Are they about to..."

"Can I finish my damn toast?" I asked, slightly disgruntled at them interrupting.

"My bad, Way," Ciji said, waving hands in my direction for me to continue. "Gon' head."

"Fuck it. We made it, drink up or whatever," I

said before lifting my flute and downing its contents in one gulp.

"Rude ass," Kalise muttered, bringing my attention to her.

"What's that?" I asked.

"All right, y'all. I'm out," Kalise said, turning to Rachel and Ciji who immediately frowned at her words.

"What? No! We're supposed to get entirely too twisted tonight to celebrate actually making this one's crazy ass timetable for this show," Ciji said, jerking a thumb in Rachel's direction.

"Hey! You said you liked a challenge," Rachel said back.

"When the challenge makes sense, Rach," Ciji insisted as the other murmured in agreement.

"At any rate, I've got an early morning with Dad, so as much as I'd love to get *twisted* as you said Ceej, I've gotta boogie."

Dejectedly the women accepted Kalise's parting hugs and air kisses without argument because we all were well-aware of her father's health concerns. One of the major reasons why Kalise had moved back to town was to take over their family business in the wake of her father's declining health. I hadn't known until my own daddy had shared the news with us that Mr. Worthington had suffered a mild, stroke-adjacent incident over the summer. Though his wife,

Kalise's stepmom, helped out with Worthington Nursery, she couldn't manage it all on her own which was why they'd summoned Kalise back home. Again, all information I'd had to find out secondhand.

"William, walk her to her car and make sure she's safe," Ciji said as Kalise walked from the group.

"Nah, Way's got it. Right, bro?" I turned my attention from where I'd been tracking her as she moved through the crowd. "Go make sure KK makes it safely to her ride, man."

"I don't think..." Ciji started, but Will cut in. "They need to work this shit out, babe."

He wasn't lying. The way we'd been around each other and not really speaking directly to each other was wild. And unlike what was my normal inclination, I'd shrank back when it came to direct conflict with Kalise, not wanting a repeat of the last time she and I had conversed. Well, that time was more like she'd screamed her head off and then slammed her door in my face as I tried pleading my case. Because time had given me the wisdom to realize that in that situation I was the only one in the wrong, I'd been hesitant in trying to get things back to the way they used to be between us. Juvenile behavior for someone who was old enough to know damn better. And my brother had been talking my head off about it for the past few months where we'd seen Kalise damn near daily and I'd still done nothing to mend the situation.

"KK, wait up," I called out as I broke into a slight jog to catch up with her before she'd completely made her way out the ballroom.

Her stride halted briefly as she turned around, realized it was me and not my twin, then pivoted to keep moving. I shook my head with a chuckle and still kept up my hurried steps to walk alongside her by the time we'd reached the building's exit.

"I'm good, Wayland," she said as I held the door open for her to precede me. "I don't need an escort. I'm parked right up front."

"Better safe than sorry," I said, still following her. "Besides, we need to talk."

"And I just said I had an early morning, so that is clearly not happening tonight," Kalise shot back immediately.

"Okay, so when?" I pressed.

"I don't know, okay. Your urgency doesn't make anything an emergency for me anymore, Wayland."

"KK, c'mon."

Before she could offer me another rebuttal, her phone sounded off and she reached to dig it out, frowning when she viewed the caller's name. Instead of responding to me, she swiped to answer.

"Alma, slow down," Kalise said. "I can't understand you."

I went on high alert because Alma was her stepmother's name and if she was calling frantically, it clearly had something to do with Kalise's father.

"Hey! Where are they taking him? No, I'm on my way home now. Is she riding with him? Do I need to...okay, okay. I'll see y'all in a bit."

The stricken look on her face as she disconnected the call immediately let me know that whatever Alma had said wasn't good. "Keys, KK."

She blinked hard like she hadn't remembered that I was standing there until her gaze focused on me.

"Where are your keys?"

Robotically she fished them from the small purse she carried. I pressed a button to unlock the doors to her car and escorted her over to the passenger side. She let me, too shell shocked to argue I guess. I rounded the car and got into the driver's seat after adjusting it back slightly, then pushed the start button on the car and drove us out of the parking lot. "Loyola?" I asked, assuming that her father had been taken to the local hospital.

Kalise nodded before dropping her head and murmuring under her breath.

With one hand I quickly tapped out a text letting my brother know that I was taking KK to the hospital and with the other I whipped her little Prius through the streets of our city at breakneck speed, praying that whatever was going on with her father wasn't something that would be fatal. He'd been recovering from his earlier medical emergency pretty well over the past few months according to my dad.

"Your daddy's taking Alma to meet them at the hospital," Kalise said, turning her gaze toward me.

"He's gonna be alright, whatever it is, KK," I said, for lack of anything better to say.

She just lowered her head and went back to murmuring under her breath. The intermittent "please Gods" that met my ears let me know that she was praying fervently. Silently I joined her, not knowing the specifics but praying that we wouldn't pull up to the hospital to bad news.

Minutes later we were at the hospital and I parked near emergency services and quickly hustled Kalise into the building. She was still eerily quiet, which lowkey unsettled me because I could only imagine what was going on in her brain. When we walked into the waiting room in the ER, I spotted my dad who came over to us immediately.

"Hey, Ladybug," he greeted Kalise, pulling her into a gentle hug. "Alma's back there with Kenny and they told me to let that nurse know when you got here. He's all right, just a little out of it."

With those words, the dam that'd been holding back whatever emotions were swirling in her mind broke as she leaned into my father full force, her entire body wracking with sobs. I felt powerless in the moment as he steadied her, banding his arms around her tightly as her knees buckled and she sobbed into his shoulder for a few minutes until she'd regained her composure. All the while my dad murmured words of reassurance in her ear as he rubbed her back comfortingly. Once she was ready to go back, he'd escorted her to the nurse's station then returned to where I sat.

"What the hell happened, Daddy?" I asked as he sank into the seat next to me.

"Not sure of all the details," he started, then shook his head. "All I knew was that one moment the cul de sac was quiet and then the next Alma was wailing louder than the damn ambulance sirens as they pulled onto the street. I came out to see what was going on and saw them loading Kenny up. I managed to calm Alma down long enough for her to tell me that she thought he was having a stroke and that she'd needed to call Ladybug. If you need to get back, I've got it here."

I cut my eyes at him incredulously and he chuckled a bit.

Jackass. He'd known exactly what he was doing with that comment.

A few moments of silence passed before my dad spoke up again. "So does you bringing her here mean that you finally fixed things between the two of you?"

I grimaced before shaking my head. "Not exactly. I just happened to be right there when she got the call. Knew I couldn't let her drive herself."

"Mmmmhmmm, " Daddy said.

"Go ahead and speak your piece, Daddy. I know you got something to say."

He just snorted and shrugged. "I'm all out of words, son. You already know how I feel about it."

Yeah, I knew how everybody felt about it. I was the bad guy. The one who'd fucked it all up. And instead of trying to avoid the hard road, I'd finally decided that I was well overdue in fixing where things had gone wrong. My timing, per usual, was shit though. So instead of lamenting about how things between KK and I had gone so off course, I poured my mental energy into praying for Big Kenny and his recovery. Losing him before she was ready had been her worst nightmare from when we were kids after she'd tragically lost her mother at a young age. The very last thing that KK needed was for things to take a bad turn with her dad.

Kalise

I took a minute before entering the triage room that the nurse had escorted me toward. Despite being assured that he was all right, I wasn't quite sure what version of my father I was going to get when I walked through that door. Alma, God bless her, had a penchant for going full on dramatic and I couldn't tell whether or not the histrionics she'd called me with were genuine or her once again going off the deep end unnecessarily. I'd barely been able to understand what she was saying outside of dad and hospital, so my heart had immediately dropped into my stomach as her words registered. Thank goodness Daddy Preston had hopped on the line to let me know that my dad was stabilized when they'd transported him, but he was unsure about what'd led to Alma calling the ambulance in the first place.

Exhaling deeply, I pushed open the door to see my dad, resting comfortably with a few machines hooked up to him. As soon as I crossed the threshold into the room, his eyes opened slowly and a sheepish grin spread across his face.

"Hey, Ladybug," his gravelly voice rang out.

"Daddy, what happened?" I breathed out as I walked to his bedside. "And where's Alma?"

"She was getting on my damn nerves so I sent her on a walk," he groused.

I shook my head at the way he was all frowned up. "How are you feeling?" I laid a hand on his thinning hair as I leaned down to press a kiss to his cheek.

"Like I wanna go home. Alma got these people in here making all this fuss just because I closed my eyes and stumbled for a lil bit."

My eyes narrowed as I tilted my head in askance. "Alma said you were unconscious when they brought you in, Daddy. That's not closing your eyes for a lil bit."

"Wasn't no need to have them people storming my house like that," he griped.

"So what? Was she supposed to let you stay knocked out until you came to? C'mon, old man. You know that's not realistic. Have you seen a doctor yet?"

My father shook his head. "Just the nurses so far. Hopefully when a doc finally sticks his head in here it's to tell me that I can go home," he grumbled.

"Unfortunately Mr. Worthington, I won't be able to tell you that," a voice sounded from over my shoulder.

I turned around to see a tall, brown-skinned man with a shock of white hair and kind eyes making his way into the room and settling on the other side of my father.

"I'm Dr. Waltman, the on-call physician in emergency services tonight," the man said, extending a hand to me.

I shook it, replying, "Kalise Worthington, daughter of who is undoubtedly about to be emergency services' biggest headache tonight."

That response garnered me another smile from the doctor as he cracked, "Well he'll be neuro's problem since we need to keep him overnight to run a few tests and make sure that tonight's episode isn't a precursor to another, more impactful, stroke."

"Aw hell," my dad grumbled. "Ain't nobody trying to be stuck up in this cold ass place again."

"Aw hell, my ass! I don't care how you feel about it, we're not leaving here until they can give me some sort of guarantee that we're not sending you home like a ticking time bomb."

"I swear I don't know who's worse, you or Alma."

And as if he'd spoken her up, she came through

the door, fussing. "I hope you done fixed your attitude now because you got one more time to go off on me for saving your fu—" She stopped abruptly once she noticed that me and a stranger were in the room.

"Naw, keep on with that shit you were talkin'," my dad piped up and I had to bite my lip from laughing aloud. "Don't change up in front of the doc."

The two of them were a mess, but they were a loving one. From the outside looking in one may think that the way they talked to one another was what the kids today called "toxic", but really shit-talking was their love language. My father had never been one to hold his tongue, something that'd led to the quick demise of his and my mother's relationship, but had bolstered his relationship with Alma because she gave it right back to him and he loved that shit.

Ignoring him she walked over with a hand extended in the doctor's direction. "Excuse my lack of manners, I'm Alma White-Worthington, the wife of this crank."

The doctor gave her a warm smile. "Nice to meet you, Mrs. Worthington. Like I was telling your daughter here, we want to keep Mr. Worthington overnight. Run a few more tests and keep abreast of his vitals to make sure that tonight's episode won't lead to a more critical one. Transport should be here within the hour to get him up to the stroke ward and his primary care physician will check in with you all when he arrives for his rotation. Until then, do you all have any questions for me?"

"Nope, even if they think they do, they don't," my dad piped up before either me or Alma could speak.

"Hush up, Kenny!" Alma scolded before turning her attention back to the doctor. "Was this… episode a stroke? Is that why he's being placed back on the stroke unit? I see his face is drooping a bit on the left. Should we be concerned?"

"From what I can gather so far, it seems like tonight's episode wasn't a full-on stroke, but a TIA. Before he's taken to the stroke ward, we're going to get him in for a CT to figure out what caused tonight's symptoms and then work out a treatment plan going forward if there is a clot or blockage that needs to be cleared in order to prevent further damage. Like I said, that's something that'll be communicated via his PCP once all of the tests that we run tonight have been assessed for diagnosis. You both are more than welcome to stay with him for now, but once he is taken upstairs, you may be asked to leave until visiting hours restart in the morning."

"Oh I'm not going anywhere and those ladies up in the stroke ward are well-aware of this fact. We've never slept apart a day in our marriage and some health issues won't be the start of that," Alma stated, matter-of-factly.

I just shook my head as the doctor looked at her with raised brows and a lowly uttered, "Alrighty then."

"Thank you for the update, Dr. Waltman," I said with a smile.

"If you all don't have any more questions for me, I'll be going now."

"Mmmmhmmm, yeah yeah, thanks for nothin', Doc," my dad grumbled.

"You're so disrespectful, Kenny," Alma chastised as the doctor took his leave.

"You really are, Daddy," I agreed.

"Oh so now the two of you are gonna gang up on me while I'm down?" my dad asked.

I just shook my head, finally letting go of the laughter I'd been holding in since Alma had first returned to the room. "What are we gonna do with him, Alma?"

She rounded the bed to pull me into a quick embrace. "I dunno, Ladybug. I'm sorry for alarming you. I was scared as all get out and didn't know what to do beyond calling nine one one, then calling you. I just didn't..." she trailed off and I squeezed her a little tighter.

"You did right. Thank you for getting him help so quickly."

"She didn't have to interrupt you at your little party for this though," my dad piped up.

"*Little* party?" Alma tutted. "How about the

wrap party for a show that's likely going to end up bringing your *little* company back into the black, Kenny. Put some respect on the work that Ladybug has done since returning home."

"Ain't nobody disrespecting, Ladybug!"

"Calm down, Daddy. I know you meant no harm." And the very last thing we needed was for him to get all worked up over this, especially without him being totally in the clear yet. "But now that I've laid eyes on you and know that you're alright, I'm gonna go ahead and head home. I'll be back up here bright and early to bring you some clothes, Alma, and to check on you, Daddy."

"Thank you, Ladybug," Alma said.

"Of course," I replied, giving her another hug, then walking over to give my dad a hug and kiss. "Love y'all."

"We love you too, Ladybug," my dad said gruffly. "And don't you forget it."

"Impossible to do so," I replied with a small smile before taking my leave.

Once outside of his room, I took a moment to steel myself against the wall right outside of his room. I closed my eyes, breathing deeply and giving it up to God that tonight's trip to the hospital wasn't the one I'd been constantly afraid of having to deal with. Ever since my stepmother had called me nearly six months ago begging me to come back home because my father's health was declining, I'd been bracing for the day when I'd get a call that he had passed on. He'd battled problems with his blood pressure and cholesterol for decades now, but it wasn't until he'd had the mini-stroke that I realized just how precarious his time left on earth could truly be.

The thought of not being nearby if something happened to him gnawed away at me, so I'd made the decision to move back. That decision had not only cost me my dream job, but also my "dream" man since he didn't want to "give up" his life in order to move back with me. Prior to everything unfolding with my father I was certain that Christian was going to be the man that I'd spend the rest of my life with. Instead he'd quickly shown me that perhaps I still had some growing to do when it came to major decision-making. At this point was my life was a recurring montage of "you put your trust in a nigga, stupid hoe how you figure" moments.

All of which had begun with being betrayed by the first guy outside of my father that I'd put all of my trust in.

The same guy who was now stationed just beyond the double doors that would lead me back to the emergency room waiting room.

The same guy who I'd purposefully been avoiding spending too much time one-on-one with because still holding onto a petty grudge for this long seemed silly in the grand scheme of things.

But I couldn't hide out in this triage hallway forever, so I needed to get over myself and get back out there. I prayed his father was still hanging around so I could foist Wayland off on him instead of having to deal with him getting back in my car with me. While I was thankful that he'd taken the initiative to make sure I'd made it here safely, tonight had been enough of an emotional rush already that I didn't want to have to deal with him on top of everything else. I let out yet another deep breath before pushing off the wall and making my way back out to the waiting room. I emerged to not only see Daddy Preston and Wayland sitting in the hard plastic chairs that made up the space but also Billy and Ciji. Ceej was actually the one who noticed my reappearance first as she rushed up to me and asked, "How's he doing, friend?"

The Preston men were quick on her heels and soon I was surrounded by a group of expectant faces.

"They don't think it was a stroke, but want to do some more testing and monitoring just to be sure. He was back there talkin' smack to Alma when I left so in my estimation he's doing just fine," I finished with a wry smile.

"Good. Good!" Ciji exclaimed.

"Y'all didn't have to leave the party," I replied

and Ciji gave me such a sharp look that if it were a knife it would have cut me.

"The hell we didn't. Everything was winding down anyway, so where else would we have been but here with you," she said.

My smile grew a little wider at those words. She and I hadn't been acquainted long, but we'd clicked almost immediately when I'd moved into the house next door to hers. I wasn't one who had a lot of friends, or let folks get super close to me, but Ciji wasn't trying to hear that at all. I high key loved the energy she'd given while bullying me into being her friend though. At the time, with moving back here and not really having anyone here that I could call friend any longer, it had been much needed. She was a listening ear or crying shoulder, whatever the occasion had called for, whenever my frustrations with my dad or Alma, and how they'd handled things from business dealings to his health, had driven me nearly to my breaking point.

"Appreciate you, sis," I said to her before turning to Daddy Preston, "Alma's gonna stay here with Daddy, so I guess your job here is done."

"Had to make sure you're good, Ladybug," he said, stepping closer to wrap me in his embrace and pressing a soft kiss to the top of my head. "I'll be to see about Kenny's hardheaded ass in the morning. Wayland, you'll make sure Ladybug gets home safe."

"Actually, we drove my car here so technically he needs a ride to his car, so if you don't—"

Daddy Preston cut me off. "I'm an old man, Ladybug. Can't be driving all over town at all hours of the night. Way will see you home. And I know Billy's gonna be right across the way, so he can kindly bring his brother home after you're all settled." He said it in such a resolute tone that I knew arguing with him would be fruitless.

"Yes, sir," I replied as he let me go and gave Ciji and his sons quick goodbyes before he'd strode out of the ER doors.

"Now Billy, you all can just—" I started, but he held up a hand.

"You ain't about to get my ass in trouble with Daddy. You heard our marching orders. Last thing I need is to walk out there and let him see you driving yourself home. Then we gotta hear about that shit for the next twenty years. He *still* gives us shit for that one time you fools were taking turns jumping out the treehouse and you broke your damn forearm. Nope. See y'all over on Maple," he replied before grabbing Ciji's hand and leading her out of the hospital. She tossed a helpless look and mouthed sorry in my direction before they disappeared behind the double doors of the ER's entrance.

I rolled my eyes and huffed a breath before looking at Wayland expectantly. "Well, c'mon, man. You got the keys," I sniped before stalking in the direction that everyone else had taken. Sure as shit, Daddy Preston was still in the parking lot under the guise of warming up his car as we passed him to get to my car. As we passed his car, he rolled down a window and yelled out, "Y'all be safe!" then pulled out of the lot.

I said nothing as I turned to Wayland and held out my hand when we were in front of my car.

"You sure you're in a condition to drive?"

"Tony, boy if you don't give me my damn keys! Bad enough I'm forced to carry you home with me because your daddy thinks somebody might snatch me up in the two miles it'll take to get from here to my house."

With a smirk he reached into the pocket of his trousers and tossed my key fob to me. I pressed the button on my door to unlock, then slid into the driver's seat, instantly annoyed.

"You couldn't move this back?"

"Had more pressing things on my mind, KK. My bad, baby."

"Don't call me that."

"KK?"

"No, the other thing."

"My bad, ba—erm, KK. Habits die hard."

I said nothing in response to that, just sucked my teeth, pressed the button to start my car, and navigated to my house. The ride there was swathed in silence since it was a short one and I didn't know where my phone was to connect it to the Bluetooth to stream any music. I was also driving like a bat out of hell to make the time I'd have to spend in this man's presence as short as I possibly could. When we were turning onto my block, he finally spoke up again.

"You know we still need to talk, right? I'm gonna give you a little bit of space because I'm sure emotions are still high from this little scare with your pops tonight, but I'm over this shit, KK. I'm done being at odds with you. So whatever we gotta do to fix this shit we're doing it."

"And if I'm perfectly fine with staying at odds with you?" I shot back, being contrary for the sake of.

Wayland snorted. "Yeah, okay."

With no further comeback shortly thereafter I was grateful to be turning into my driveway, noticing that Will's SUV was idling in front of Ciji's place. I hopped out of my car, striding toward my front door when I heard Way speak up again. "Your bag," he said from not too far behind me, as he jogged in my direction. "I'd put it in the glove box while we were inside." I was in such a rush to get out of this man's presence that I hadn't even thought about my belongings.

"Thanks," I murmured before turning back toward my door and inputting the combination to unlock my door on the keypad.

"KK," Way called out.

I didn't respond in any way beyond stopping my stride through the front door with my shoulders set, almost as if I were bracing for some sort of impact. He didn't disappoint when he walked right up on me, resting his hands on the frame of my door as he leaned forward to speak directly into my ear.

"For what it's worth, and this is overdue, I'm sorry, Kalise. I made the most egregious error in judgment and lost one of the most important people in my life because she dared to look out for me. You gotta at least give me a shot to make it up to you."

I turned around to see sincerity in his gaze as he stared down at me, halting the flippant "I ain't gotta do anything but stay Black and die" that was on the tip of my tongue. That sincerity coupled with the fact that I was over carrying this grudge and could really use my friend again was what led to me instead responding with, "We'll talk later."

His eyes squinted as his gaze bore into me a little deeper, which made me squirm under the intense scrutiny.

"For real, Tony. We'll talk. Give me a little bit of time." My usage of the childhood nickname I'd given him landed as intended when the corners of his eyes crinkled and his lips turned up slightly.

"Aight, you got it. But I mean what I said. We're fixing this shit, *soon*," Way insisted.

I let out a shallow breath at the persistence of his tone.

"I heard you," I said in response.

"Sweet dreams, KK," he murmured before turning and leaving me to watch him make his way down the path that led to my front door.

"Ni-night, Tony," I whispered, barely audible enough for him to hear me.

Wayland

"That looked pretty intense, bruh," Will said as I got into the passenger side of his car.

"Not talking about this with you right now."

"Oooh, somebody's testy. Ain't that a bitch. Like you're the one being made to be the errand boy right now instead of being laid up with his lady."

"I coulda called a rideshare, bro."

"And then took your ass out to Daddy's crying about it tomorrow, which would have made him call me talking shit. Nah, man. I don't think so."

"Damn shame a man is so scared of his father at this advanced age."

"Hmph, you're one to talk since I see you're finally making a real effort to get things right with KK after Daddy spent most of tonight lighting into your ass in that waiting room about it."

I thought I'd gotten somewhat of a reprieve from my father talking to me about the rift between me and KK, but the longer we'd sat in the waiting room, I guess the more his patience had waned so he finally let go of everything he'd been wanting to say to me about that whole situation go. Billy and Ciji had walked in just when he had hit his stride while chewing me out, something the two of them were a little too amused by.

"Thanks for having my back then, by the way," I grumbled.

"Say, were you not the same one who gave me shit when I was denying why Ciji had me so hot under the collar?"

"You wear draws with collars?"

"Watch it, fam," Will said, laughing.

"Shiiiiid, I'm just saying. I know where you were hot for ol' Miss Sinclair and I ain't never heard of boxers with collars. I was just asking for clarity's sake."

"And that's why I let Daddy go in on your ass earlier. You deserved it."

"Cold world when your own twin can't even have your back."

"Hey, whenever you're right, I'm rolling with you. But your ass was beyond wrong when you took Crissa's side over KK's, Way. I still don't know what that girl put on you to have your ass caught up over her the way you were."

"She used to do this crazy shit with her tongue, g."

"Your ass ain't ever serious," Will replied, laughing.

"Nah, for real. She had seemingly damning evidence that made me believe her over KK. It wasn't until well after everything between us blew up that I'd realized how much of that shit was straight up fabricated, but by then?" I shrugged. "Everything was too far gone. KK was halfway across the country and not responding to any of the multitude of ways I'd tried reaching out to her. And... well I never told anyone this before because the shit was embarrassing, but Big Kenny had reached out to me and asked that I stop harassing his Ladybug."

"Oh shit, not her siccing her pops on you. Wait... is that why he played us when I approached him about Worthington being our sole supplier?"

"We were years past all of this by then, but... yeah probably."

"Damn, no wonder you never went and had that face to face with him like I'd asked you to several times and instead found us someone else to supplement the scraps that we got from Worthington. Not that I'm mad about the nursery out in Orchard Lake supplying us because they haven't let us down yet. But hey... if you get back on good terms with KK, you need to see about us getting better terms and conditions with Worthington and exclusivity. Cultivating relationships with a local vendor is always better, man."

"Wow, not you caring more about our damn botanical supply relationships than me getting back the only woman I've ever..." I trailed off, realizing that I'd already said too much.

"The only woman you've ever..." my twin echoed.

"Nothing, man," I responded quickly, thankful that we'd pulled up to the venue where my car was the last one sitting in the parking lot. "Thanks again for the ride, bro. I'll holler at you later." I didn't give him a chance to respond before I was hopping out of his car and into my own.

Once I got home, I couldn't stop thinking about the events of the evening. Despite having gone into tonight knowing that I'd wanted to mend the rift with KK, I hadn't thought that it was a feasible goal with the way she'd been icing me out since we'd been back in each other's orbits. Now that I knew I had somewhat of an in, I knew that I needed to take advantage of it. In a perfect world, I'd not only be able to put myself back in her good graces, but would also hope that someday she would be interested in the possibility of pursuing something more? It felt crazy to say, but I'd been in love with her ever since I'd discovered her crying in my backyard treehouse when we were eleven years old.

KK had just moved to live with her father full-time and it was an adjustment period for her to say the least. Though she'd visited him for extended summer breaks and the occasional holiday, she wasn't used to being under her father's care on a permanent basis. Our daddy had told us about her impending move and that she'd lost her mother, so that my brother and I could take care of how we dealt with her as she was still grieving. Since we'd been motherless from birth, we could relate in some ways. Granted the depth of her hurt was more acute since she'd actually spent significant time with her mother as the most prominent caregiver in her life. The night I'd discovered her in the treehouse was well after both of our bedtimes. I could hear what sounded like sniffles coming from the treehouse through my open window so I'd snuck out of the house to investigate. Luckily I'd learned how to be pretty stealth when sneaking out because if my daddy had caught me that night it would have been my ass.

Kalise had been all up in arms because that night her father had introduced her to his lady friend. She was convinced that he was trying to quickly replace her mother in her life and she'd left the house in a fit, wanting to run away but without money or a clear-cut plan, her options on where to go were few. She'd planned on hiding out in the treehouse 'til morning and hopefully coming up with a plan for living on her own going forward. After I'd spent hours talking her down from becoming a real life Boxcar child, she and I had fallen asleep in the treehouse and were rudely awakened by both of our fathers going slam off about us not being where we should have been, tightly ensconced in our respective beds. I'd instantly taken the blame for us both, not wanting to see Kalise in any more pain than I'd already witnessed her dealing with. I'd gotten grounded for two weeks, but it was worth it just knowing that I'd been there for her when she'd needed someone. While I was on lockdown, she'd sent little notes to me through Will and when I finally was free again, she and I became thick as thieves.

Whereas previously there had been just Will and me, we'd now become a threesome. Though most times Will would just leave the two of us together, claiming that he didn't like being the third wheel. Both KK and I had insisted that he was being silly because we weren't thinking about one another in any way beyond friendship.

That'd been the first time that I lied to her... and myself.

It wasn't until we were seniors in high school that I realized that the intense emotional connection and innate sense of protection that I had with and for KK wasn't just because she was my best friend outside of my brother. My feelings for her had run deeper than I knew how to properly articulate at the time, so I never did. Instead, I kept myself in the friend zone, never wanting to rock the boat. All of the girls I'd dated during this time could see right through me though. It was why no relationship that I'd entered into truly worked. It wasn't until we'd gone to separate colleges, so we weren't in each other's back pockets as much, that I'd finally been able to "get over" KK. We were still as close as we could be with the distance that separated us during undergrad, but when we'd all moved back to our hometown there was a distinct shift in how we interacted.

I'd brought back a girl, Crissa, with whom I'd gotten pretty serious in undergrad to live with me while my brother and I were trying to get our house flipping business off the ground. KK had been casually dating, but not settled down with anyone in particular. The first time that she and Crissa had met was actually decent though. We'd all gone out—me, Crissa, my brother and the girl he was dating at the time, KK and some guy she'd been kicking it with that we'd all gone to high school with. Everyone had a good time, or so I'd thought. When we got home Crissa was grilling me about KK, swearing that she had a feeling about her, but I brushed her off, knowing that Kalise had never seen me in any romantic light.

More and more Crissa grew increasingly antagonistic toward KK, claiming that Kalise had been lightweight stalking her in regard to me. Then she showed me screenshots of texts that, instead of blindly believing Crissa, I should have given KK the benefit of the doubt of explaining. I went in guns blazing, lobbing accusations at KK out of left field, not even giving her the chance to rebut any of them. In retrospect, and after a little bit of therapy, I came to the conclusion that I'd gone so hard because it felt to me in that moment like she hadn't found me worthy of even considering in any way beyond platonic until someone else had seen something in me.

A really fucked up state of mind to be in, honestly.

What had really hurt, however, was when KK had reminded me of a pact we'd made as children, to always have each other's back no matter what anyone else said or did to try and break our foundation down and how I'd gone against that for, in her words, "some pussy from a bottom-feeding bitch". The sentiment, while resonantly harsh, also held some truth to it in hindsight.

At first I'd found Crissa's enthusiasm about my successes to be positive, but after a while I began to notice that she had no desire to be successful in her own right. She hadn't finished undergrad like she was supposed to when we'd moved back to my hometown. The plan had been for her to transfer to a local university and finish out her coursework. Instead she just made constant references to what I would be able to do for her once I'd reached my pinnacle of success and how she didn't need a degree to be everything I needed her to be at home. The shit with KK was just the beginning of the end, honestly. I'd stayed with Crissa for far too long, thinking that she was my meant to be.

And it wasn't until damn near a year after everything had blown up and KK was once again living states away that I'd realized the error of my ways. It'd taken my damn pops looking at the so-called damning evidence and pointing out the color of the message bubbles being wrong. That led to me confronting Crissa who had broken down immediately. She'd confessed to making it all up because she was insecure about our relationship after seeing Kalise and I together. I had been so flabbergasted by the shit at the time I couldn't do shit but immediately drop Crissa's immature ass and then try to at least get KK to talk to me again so I could explain where I'd gone wrong.

And I thought once I explained we'd be able to get back on track. I even flew my ass out to where she was staying to plead my case, but instead she'd given me the breadth of her ass to kiss. And told her Daddy to take care of her lightweight when I refused to give up.

Now here we were, a few years past it all and I

was now seeing the slightest sliver of hope that if nothing else, I would at least be able to get things back on track with my *friend*.

Truth be told I'd missed the fuck out of KK. She was actually the first person to know about my passion for doing this house flipping shit. My brother and I had taken summer jobs helping out our old man at multiple construction sites in our junior and senior years of high school. At first I'd been reticent, but learning about the intricacies of construction appealed to my inner mister fix it. My brother had not loved any parts of the manual labor aspects at all. I remembered he couldn't wait to get back to school so we'd be relieved of the duties that came along with our summer gigs. I'd spend hours with KK in that backyard treehouse going on and on about all of the cool shit I'd been learning on the job sites. Prior to her encouraging me to study construction to be able to go into business for myself in the future, I'd been planning to go to college and get the easiest degree that required the least amount of work just to say I'd had one. Kalise sowed into my passions and desires, pumping me up to believe that there wasn't a thing I couldn't do.

That kind of energy, specifically from a woman who cared deeply about me, had been sorely lacking in my life as of late.

I also couldn't help but think about just how much everything she was going through with her dad had to be a lot to bear. Last I'd heard, before she'd moved back and secondhand through my dad, was that she was shacking up with some dude while teaching botany courses at the prestigious university from which she'd received her masters and doctoral degrees. She'd always made no bones about wanting to one day teach botany, despite her father being insistent that she would one day come back home and take over the family business. And she'd been living her dream until the pressing issue of his declining death had forced her back here. I wasn't quite certain what had happened with the guy she'd been with, but I had known that her pops wasn't really fond of ol' boy. My daddy had met him once and wasn't that impressed either, something he couldn't wait to share with me and rub it in. Because despite the fact that I'd never shared with anyone that I'd harbored unrequited feelings for KK, somehow my daddy had always known. And he never missed an opportunity to throw in my face about how I'd fumbled supremely when it came to KK.

Speaking of the devil, my phone began to ring and when I looked over at the display, it was him calling.

"Good morning, old man."

"Morning, son. You made sure Ladybug made it home safely last night?"

"Yes, sir," I responded.

"Good, I'm on my way to the hospital to see about Kenny and wanted to make sure you did what needed to be done."

"Tell Big Kenny and Miss Alma I said what's up."

"Mmmmhmmm. You do what I told you to, yet?"

I sighed, shaking my head at his persistence. "I'm working on it, Daddy."

"Don't work on it, son. Get it done."

"I can't make her do anything she doesn't want to do."

"Damn, between you and that other rockheaded little negro, I swear you would think that I didn't raise either one of you with any gumption. Fact of the matter is son, you need to put in more effort. I told you when you were fifteen years old that Ladybug was gonna be my daughter and you ain't managed to make that happen yet. Whew, thank God Debbi ain't here to see how her sons are out here just disappointing their old man."

"Daddy!" I exclaimed. "Did you really just invoke the name of my dead mother to emphasize my *alleged* shortcomings?"

"If that's what it takes to light a fire under your ass, then I'll do what I gotta do. The one thing I know for certain is that neither one of you have been able to make anything shake with anyone else. Now, if that don't mean it's because y'all are soulmates, then I don't know what it does mean."

"You're such a sap, old man."

"Damn right. I'm getting up in age and neither of you boys have made me a grandfather yet. Hell, Kenny and I were in competition at first until we realized that we should be combining our efforts instead of trying to divide and conquer."

"I'm not entertaining this conversation anymore, Daddy. I gotta get ready for my day. I'll holler at you later."

"Aight boy, gon' head and miss ya beat again if you want to."

"Bye, Daddy. Love you."

"Love your stubborn ass too, Wayland," he declared before hanging up on me.

Rude ass.

But the last thing he'd said before hanging up kept ringing in my mind long after we'd gotten off that call. About him and Big Kenny combining their efforts. I wondered more about that, but knew that if I asked him he'd just be cagey and obfuscate. I thought about hitting up my brother to see if he had any ideas about how those two have been conspiring to get me and KK together, but if I knew nothing else about my brother I knew that he'd dropped me off last night and headed straight back to be laid up under Ciji. Shit, at least that's where I would be right now if I had the option of being laid up with my woman instead of languishing in my lonely ass space.

I wonder what KK is doing.

As quickly as the thought passed through my mind, it skittered out of it. I needed to be smart, approach reconciliation with her gently and not do too much. Coming on too strong would garner me the exact opposite of the outcome I wanted. This was knowledge I'd long held. KK wasn't a fan of guys who were on what she called "team too much", the zero to a hundred, balls to the wall type. She much preferred to ease into friendships and relationships, letting them flourish on a natural progression and not trying to force things to happen quicker than they'd naturally occur.

In our case, the ball was now in her court. I'd laid my stance bare for her last night, letting her know where I stood and she'd said that we would talk. I knew not to press her, but I hoped for damn sure that she would be getting in contact with me sooner rather than later. I hadn't been a direct recipient of it as of late, but there was a special sort of kinetic energy that just emanated from Kalise in whatever space she was in. Folks flocked to her easily because of that energy, a brilliant sort of light that shone out to others as a beacon that being in her presence was a safe haven. Through Will I'd learned that she and Ciji had become fast friends, building a relationship that felt like it'd been forged for years instead of the mere months that they had known one another.

That was something I'd found both fascinating

and also encouraging. Her being so open to bonding with Ciji gave me a sliver of hope that all wasn't lost when it came to us rekindling. That even though she'd been holding onto the tension that had become commonplace between us, maybe there was a shot for me to salvage what we'd shared from the fossilized remains of our former relationship. Hell, for all I knew, perhaps this time spent apart hadn't completed obliterated our bond, but instead had formed a chrysalis around the tenuous strands that remained, cobbling them together for an undetermined amount of time only for us to reemerge as something new, something renewed.

"Aight, g. Enough of these fucking musings, get your ass up and get a workout in today," I grumbled to myself under my breath.

Of the two of us, my brother was always thought to be the more rigid, stuck in the mud type, but quiet as kept I too was a sucker for my routines. I didn't like to get thrown too far off track if I could help it, especially when it came to my fitness. I wasn't a muscle head, gym rat, but I did take daily movement seriously. Either running a few miles daily or doing some sort of full body workout in my home gym. Today was actually a run day, so I got dressed in running gear, cued up my running playlist, strapped my phone to my bicep, threw in my AirPods and set off to take a three mile run through my neighborhood. Though I varied the route incrementally, I tended to pass by the same streets and intersections at some point during the run.

Along the way I waved to neighbors that were out sitting on porches or walking their pets as I pounded the pavement, with a medley of rap songs from my teenage and adult years as the soundtrack for the run. So much for getting KK off my mind, I thought as the opening strains "U Don't Know" by Jay Z started up and instantly I was transported back to when we were in high school and I'd convinced her pops to let me surprise her with tickets to see Jay live in concert for her birthday. She'd been a superfan of his for years, but had never seen him live so when the opportunity presented itself I'd hopped on that shit as quickly as I could. I'd spent all of my little coins to make sure we had dope ass seats, not on the floor, but on the one hundred levels, right in the very first rows, not too far from the stage.

That night had been one for the books too since one of my homies from school had a cousin who worked at the venue where the concert was being held and had managed to finesse us a couple of passes to get in early and check out Jay's soundcheck as well as do a radio station meet and greet where KK had muffed the hell out of another girl to make sure that she was plastered to one of Jay's sides in the group photo we'd taken with him before the show. She'd also sworn that during "Girls Girls

Girls" he'd looked her way, waved and winked. As we were leaving the show, she told everyone who would listen about the special bond she and Jay had shared with hundreds of feet, and thousands of people, between them. The way she'd buzzed with excitement all throughout that night had me feeling like the man.

Hell in the ensuing days and months later, she bragged on how I'd treated her to the best night of her life and that I was one of the best parts of her life and that she was so thankful for our friendship. Her gratitude was something I'd carried with me for years after, knowing that I'd been the one to make her as happy as I'd ever seen her had my chest poked out with pride. I'd give up almost anything to evoke that sort of feeling in her once again. KK deserved the world as far as I was concerned and I'd be willing to move heaven and earth to give it to her.

As I was on my way back home on the tail end of my run, an uber-familiar, sweet smell wafted through the air as I passed Sweet Thang Patisserie. Feeling like my nose had to be deceiving me, I doubled back and made my way into the bakery, hoping like hell I wasn't too ripe from my run.

"Hi, welcome to Sweet Thang, when you're ready to order just let me know?" a voice chirped as I crossed the threshold.

"You guys got sticky buns in here?" I asked.

"Will?" a male voice called out as he walked

through the double doors leading from the back of the bakery.

I turned to see my old neighbor's youngest son. "Nah Dame, it's Way," I said, extending a hand in his direction for a shake.

I hadn't seen him in years, but seeing his face confirmed that my nose had not, in fact, deceived me.

"This you?" I asked, gesturing to the place. I'd passed by it plenty of times but had never thought to stop in. I wasn't huge on sweets like that, only indulging in a few items sparingly.

"Yeah," he said with a nod. "Been operating here for a few years now."

"Using your moms' recipes?"

He grinned. "A few of 'em here and there. Actually I just added her famous sticky buns as an offering since I finally perfected them after too many years of trial and error."

"I knew it!" I damn near yelled. "I need parts of those, my guy."

Dame chuckled, moving behind one of the glass cases and pulling out a tray lined with them. "Say less, man. How many?"

"Let's start with four, but knowing KK we'll likely be back for more soon."

"You finally got your shit together and got the girl, huh? I see you, lil bruh."

"Not exactly," I hedged. "But these..." I said,

holding up the pink bakery box that he'd slid across the counter to me. "Might go a long way in making that a reality real soon. What's my damage?"

"For an old friend, this one's on the house. Just promise me you won't be a stranger out here. Come back with ya twin and post my shit up on your Instagram. Wife's a big fan of the show, so I know she'd love to meet you both."

"And a little promo from the hometown heroes ain't never hurt nobody," I tossed in.

"Exactly, you feel me. I mean we ain't hurting for business, but ain't nothin wrong with a little boost every now and again."

"I hear you, fam. I'll coordinate with bro and figure out when we can come back and meet the wife and all that."

"Here," Dame said, reaching into his wallet and handing me a card. "Call me directly and we can get it worked out since I'm typically not in this location as often since I'm trying to get the one across town up and running soon."

"Bet. Good seeing you, my guy."

"Same here, tell your pops I said what's good," Dame said as I exited his bakery.

Between the Jay Z reminiscence and then randomly happening upon what used to be one of our favorite treats as shorties whenever Mrs. Patterson made them to share with neighbors, I had to stop faking the funk and put myself back in

Kalise's presence as soon as possible. It seemed like a deluge of signs from the universe that I no longer needed to slow roll this mending and act with fervor. I just hoped that I wouldn't be coming on too strong and risking ending the resolution before it began.

Kalise

The sound of my doorbell interrupted my cool down sequence after my yoga workout and I was tempted to just let whoever was ringing it just sit there until I came back into my body. I'd recently taken up the practice to help alleviate the massive amounts of stress I'd been under from moving back to my hometown. My dad's health coupled with the fact that our family business was on the skids really did me no favors considering that I'd also been staring down the barrel of the demise of my relationship. Realistically I'd known that Christian wasn't that guy. But I'd tried like hell to overlook his shortcomings and make something shake between us regardless.

What a fool's mission that had been because I set myself up for a heartbreak far greater than one I could have avoided had I just listened to my gut in the first place. Dad had never liked him on the couple of occasions that they'd met and neither had Alma. Dad not really liking him didn't mean much because he wasn't a fan of any boy or man that I'd brought around who was trying to court me. But Alma having her misgivings was the most massive red flag that I ignored because I felt like I was at a time in my life where settling down and committing to a man was the next step of my life's master plan. I'd achieved professional acclaim through being published in some of the most prestigious journals in my discipline. I was on track to become tenured at the institution for which I taught. So naturally, this man, who I'd already given a few of my life's best years already was meant to be one who would stick around for the long haul.

Never mind the fact that he complained about my dedication to my work, while being wholly consumed to the point of distraction with his.

Never mind the fact that he would never give me a straight answer about wanting kids or a family despite me constantly saying that was one of my most ardent goals.

Never mind the fact that he was estranged from and had never introduced me to anyone in his family.

The last one was the most critical considering that we'd lived in his hometown area and I'd made the effort to integrate him into the life of my loved ones as deeply as our lives were enmeshed. In the three years that Christian and I had dated I'd yet to meet anyone who had known him any longer than I had. In the end I'd learned that was purposeful.

Shaking off that journey my mind decided to travel down as I weighed opening the door or not, I decided not to be a jackass and at least see who it was. Most likely it was Ciji, who had been watching my interaction with Wayland last night like a hawk. Since she and Will were tied together at the hip she'd been on me heavily, trying to make fetch happen with me and Way. I'd had to tell her several times that despite what she may have thought, he and I were never romantically inclined or involved. And that was God's honest truth. Despite how close we were at one point in time, I'd never really looked at him as more than my best friend. Objectively, I knew that he—and his brother—were both handsome, to say the least, fine as hell if we were being a bit more accurate, and raised by a village who'd ensured that whatever women were lucky enough to end up with either of them would be treated like royalty.

But I also knew the risk that if I'd even thought about crossing that line and it didn't work out, then I'd ruin one of the most precious connections I'd ever had in life. And I'd thought he felt the same way, but he'd proven me wrong.

I also had to admit though that I missed the hell

out of my friend. In a perfect world, the little rift that'd occurred between us wouldn't have lasted long enough to create the chasm that now existed between us. But egos, hurt feelings, and plain ol' stubbornness that I'd rightfully inherited from my dad said otherwise. As time had marched on though, my stance had softened a bit, but I wasn't going to be the first one to break. Thankfully for me, last night he had been the one to make the first step to mending our relationship. Of course I couldn't make it too easy for him because when all was said and done the way he'd carelessly tossed away our decades of context for some jealous skip skap had really done a number on me. I'd already had a time really letting folks get too close for fear of losing them. So to have my best friend, the one person who, above all, was supposed to always have *my* back choose someone else over me? Yeah that shit stung more than a little bit.

Sighing, I finally got up from my yoga mat, ready to tell Ceej to mind her business and leave me alone about Way. When I opened the door, however, I was surprised to find someone else on my stoop.

"What are you doing here?" I asked, semi-breathlessly.

Way smiled that brilliant white grin of his that'd gotten him out of more shit than a little bit throughout his years on earth before his piercing gaze slowly scanned my form and made me feel like the yoga tights and sports bra that I was currently wearing was something more scandalous. He remained silent as a wolfish gleam came and went in his gaze so quickly that I damn near felt like I'd imagined it. I shifted uncomfortably, not certain what to do with this markedly different energy that was flowing between us now.

"Hello?" I prompted and he shook his head, letting out a small chuckle.

"My bad. Morning, KK. You'll never guess what I've managed to get my hands on this morning," he replied, holding up a pink bakery box and taking a step toward me like I'd invited him in.

"Am I missing something here?" I asked, not moving as he stepped a little too deep into my personal space.

"You're gonna miss out on this sweet treat I got for you if you keep playin'," he jibed before sliding between the incremental space I'd left between myself and the door frame.

The slight graze of his body past mine sent a tremor of... something I couldn't quite identify through me.

Instead of interrogating that any further, I shut the door, turned on my heel and followed in the wake of the path Wayland had taken into my kitchen. He was perched on one of the stools in front of my center island, awaiting my presence. Once I stood on the other side of the island from him, he said, "I bet if I gave you a million guesses you'd never guess what's in here," as he drummed his fingers atop the bakery box.

"So are you just gonna tell me?"

"Well, first...you got any decent coffee in here or nah?"

"Wayland Anthony Preston!"

"Damn, the full name? I'm in trouble?"

"I've asked this already and you know how much I hate repeating myself. I'm going to give you the benefit of the doubt that you didn't hear me the first time. So, I'll ask again. What are you doing here?"

"Remember, we're supposed to be mending fences. Getting things back to the way they're supposed to be? You agreed to it."

"I also remember asking you to give me a bit of time."

"Oh, sleeping on it wasn't long enough?" he asked, giving me a cheeky grin.

I rolled my eyes. "Don't think you're slick. I know what you're doing with the million-dollar smile and the charm and the," I trailed off, waving my hand in an abstract motion toward his general direction.

"And the...?" he prompted.

"Wayland!"

"Oh you for real irritated, huh? Fine, fine. Open this up then and I promise you won't regret letting me in," he said as he slid the bakery box in my direction.

"I don't recall letting you anywhere," I grumbled as I snatched the box toward me and lifted the top to see… "No way," I breathed out. "Where did you… How did you… Are these?"

"Mrs. Patterson's famous sticky buns? Yep, sure are."

"But she's been gone…God rest her soul…for a good five or so years, ain't no way these are made by her," I replied, turning from the counter to grab a saucer from the cabinets.

"Remember Dame, her youngest? He owns a bakery now. Though, he bougie as hell so he calls it a patisserie. *Anyway*, I smelled the buns when I was out for a run and thought my nose was playing tricks on me. Popped in the bakery, chopped it up with Dame who confirmed that he'd finally perfected his mama's recipe and the rest is history. So whassup, you got some coffee or nah?"

"I mean, you couldn't bring that with you? If this is supposed to be an olive branch to restoring our friendship and everything."

"Damn, it's like that, KK?"

"What did you expect, Wayland?" I sassed.

"Can you stop calling me that? I'm halfway expecting you to tell me to go grab a switch every time you say my name."

"What am I supposed to call you if not your name?"

"Don't be obtuse, KK."

Instead of responding to that, I plated one of the sticky buns and stuck it into the microwave to heat up for a quick twenty seconds, then rooted through my silverware drawer for a fork once I took it back out. Whole time, I was being watched with a hyper-scrutinizing stare that seemed to burrow through all the layers of cells to the core of me. I tried like hell to ignore him as I retrieved my sticky bun and dug into it, but the energy was just too... much to deny.

"What, Tony?" I snapped as I lifted my eyes back to meet his.

"There we go! Progress..." he said, clapping before he moved around to complete the same plating, microwaving, and digging in cycle that I had with another of the buns.

We ate for a few moments in silence before he spoke up again.

"So, I'm taking it there's no coffee here?"

"It's the way you not only barged in here uninvited but got the nerve to be making demands. What makes you think you've got rights in this house?"

"That's a no then?"

"You're so irritating. Maybe I shouldn't be so quick to give you a chance to get back in my good graces," I teased before going over and taking out my Nespresso machine and making us a couple of lattes.

"Thank you, KK."

"Yeah yeah," I fake-grumbled, secretly pleased at the way we'd sort of fallen right back into the dynamic that suited us best.

I finished up my sticky bun and it took everything in me not to go back into the box for a second one. I'd have to roll over to the bakery on my own time to stock up on these buns though. It'd easily been a good ten plus years since I'd had one of these. Mrs. Patterson used to make them for every occasion —holiday potlucks, block parties, birth of a baby, funerals, it didn't matter. And any opportunity that I saw them up for grabs, I'd always snag two minimally —one for me, one for Tony.

I let out a sigh and then said, "Can I ask you something? And I need you to be perfectly honest with me."

"Anything," he replied.

"Why were you so quick to throw me away over that Crissa chick?"

"I didn't throw—" he started, but I interrupted, raising a hand. "You absolutely were throwing me away with the way you came to me over some mess. You didn't even give me a chance to say anything while you went off the deep end about how convenient it was that I wanted you when you had somebody who you wanted. Like, what the fuck was that? And to act like I was harassing that girl? When at no point in time had I ever even given you the idea that I wanted to be anything more than just your friend. Because, let's be clear, we were as close as two could possibly be but the one thing I thought we'd agreed on, over all things, was that we would never even think about ruining our friendship if attraction became too much to bear. And I damn sure wouldn't have called myself sabotaging your relationship! I mean, honestly, Tony. That's what hurt my feelings *the most*, that you thought I could be capable of something so underhanded. That I would stoop to going behind your back and hurting you before keeping it real with you."

"I wasn't thinking, that was the problem. I messed everything up simply because I let my own ego get in the way."

"What does that even mean?"

He ran his hand atop his head, a true tell that he was growing uncomfortable with the progression of the conversation. He mumbled something under his breath before looking up at me with a stricken sort of look in his eyes. "All this time and you still can't see it."

"W-what are you talking about?" I stammered.

"The fact that I've been in love with you since we were eleven years old, KK. The fact that the reason I was so quick to believe the accusations that Crissa levied on you was because then it made me feel like less of a loser for pining after you with no feelings in return that whole time. Haven't you ever wondered why, despite the fact of dating plenty of girls I'd never settled down? Could never fully commit to them? Crissa was the first time that I could see myself actually being in it for the long haul with someone without your unwitting interference. But then she showed me those texts and I got angry, because instead of coming to me and telling me your feelings, you were more comfortable going behind my back and trying to ruin what had been, to me at the time anyway, the most solid relationship of my young adult life. Which made me question whether or not you truly wanted me or just didn't want anyone else to have me while you strung me along. Or whether it took someone else seeing the value in me before you could allow yourself to see it too. Either of those outcomes pretty much cemented you as public enemy number one in my eyes. Which made it easy for me to go off the deep end."

"Tony, I..." I trailed off, truly speechless. Hell if he'd given me a million guesses I would have never presumed either of those things to be true.

He chuckled humorlessly after a few more moments of silence passed. "I'ma raise up outta here, Kalise."

His usage of my full name caused me to snap to attention as he began to make his way back toward my front door. "Wait, what?" I asked.

"I... this was a mistake. You said you needed some time to settle into us being back in each other's lives again and I shouldn't have pushed the issue by coming over here today. That's my bad. I'ma... I'ma go. Give you some space to process and... yeah."

Before I could open my mouth to say anything in return or stop him, he'd already exited my house and was halfway into his car and all I could think was, *what the fuck was that?*

I sat in my house for a few hours after I'd showered and redressed, and ate another of those sticky buns, replaying everything Tony had dropped on me earlier. I hadn't the slightest clue that he'd felt anything deeper for me than the friendship we'd shared. Though, I should have been able to pick up on it through his actions, even if he could never find the words to say something to me about it.

And honestly, the biggest question that loomed in my mind was him asking if I'd ever wondered why he could never fully commit to any of the girls I'd known him to date. And while I'd never quite had the thought about his level of commitment, I'd certainly questioned my own—year over year. I kept meeting men who seemed like they had potential, could be as close to "the one" as I could get in life, but there was always something that kept me from going all in, putting all my eggs in one basket. It was something I'd previously chalked up to my fear of losing those with whom I grew closest, but now... I wondered if it was something deeper than that. Like I somehow knew on a cellular level that I'd been just biding time with the other men I'd dated in the past because it was supposed to be Tony, despite me constantly saying I never saw him that way. Was I putting a double whammy on myself by forcibly restricting him to the friend zone? This shit had me all twisted up in knots as I twirled every possible scenario over and over in my mind before finally picking up my phone and sending out an SOS text.

Gratefully not only was Ciji available, but she'd come bearing gifts in the form of hard alcohol. A slight departure from our norm of getting wine girl wasted, but one I wholeheartedly welcomed.

"Girl from the way you sounded on that text, I felt like we needed the whole bar, but we could start with ringing the bell and I can always go back over to my place if we need to reup," she said with a grin as she waltzed into my place holding up a bottle of Clase Azul. "Now you just tell me, is this a classy and glassy situation or should I just hand over this bottle and then tip back home to get one of my own?"

"As appealing as getting totally hammered instead of reconciling my feelings sounds, I'll go grab a couple glasses. You just get settled in the den."

I ended up grabbing glasses, a couple of drink mixers, and a couple bags of Sun Chips that I had in the pantry so we wouldn't be too worse for the wear as I spilled my guts.

"Alright, girlie," Ciji said once we'd each poured a few ounces worth of tequila in the squat glasses I'd brought out. "Now what the hell happened with you and Way? I promise I'll hold my 'I told you so' until you get it all out."

I rolled my eyes before launching into a brief recap of the conversation that I'd had with him earlier. And, unlike I would have normally done, I didn't hold back from expressing how I'd felt in the wake of it—the conflicting feelings that'd been warring within me all afternoon into this evening. When I finished, Ciji remained quiet, just looking at me over the rim of her glass while she sipped the last of the tequila in it.

"You're too quiet right now," I said when she said nothing after a stretch of a few moments more. "Why are you so quiet right now?"

"I... hm," Ciji started, then paused. "I'm trying to make sure that I say this...right."

"Just say it plain," I replied. " I don't need any sugar coating."

"Okay, so check it. If I'm reading this right, you're just trying to go from not having spoken to this man in x amount of years to now what, hopping into a relationship with him? Just zero to a hundred real quick, huh?"

"I didn't... that's not what... wait a damn minute, you were the one pushing for this so hard. Saying that there was clearly some underlying tension between us. I thought you'd be pushing me toward Tony instead of away from him."

"I'm not doing either, quite yet. Look. I don't have all of the years of context that you have with the twins, but from being around them this past half a year I've picked up on some things. Things of which you're already likely intimately familiar. They're incredible men, right? Like just on an interpersonal level. They were raised right, with morals, values, and all of that. A catch for any lady who's lucky and got the right lure. However, I think this thing between the two of you is more complex than you all just flipping a switch and trying to get back the KK and Tony of yesteryear. Y'all have both lived a lot of life without each other and should, essentially, not be those same two kids who'd been inseparable when you were younger."

"I mean, duh. There would be an adjustment period but like…"

"I wasn't done speaking, Kalise."

"My bad," I said, holding my hands up for her to continue.

"While I'd love to tell you to go full steam ahead because the double dates with the four of us would definitely be fire, I think that you all should ease into this new phase of your relationship with one another. Don't let deciding to potentially pursue him as a romantic interest be a reflexive action based on what you think he wants. Take the time to really get to know Wayland, the grown man, instead of Tony, your lil homeboy. And vice versa. Introduce him to grown woman you instead of lil KK from next door. Discover the things about each other that resemble those kids you once were, but also the things that have brought you to be the people who you are currently. Don't cheat it. Take the time to let it naturally blossom into what it's going to be. Not only for your sake, but his as well. Don't let the nostalgia of what you think coulda woulda shoulda been the driving force in exploring in the current day."

"This is rich coming from the woman who couldn't wait to drop down and get her eagle on for the man who is currently glued to her hip."

"Nah," Ciji said, shaking her head, "I don't think so. Our situations are completely different. I could have never imagined that I would have found one of the most meaningful and satisfying relationships of my life with Will. I was in it purely to get on his nerves and also rock his world." She tittered briefly before sobering. "But this... this thing with you and Way...or Tony as you call him. It's different. And, if I'm keeping it a bean, it has the potential for a deeper fallout if it isn't approached in the right way. Something that I know neither of you want to be the end result."

"I hear you but..." I trailed off with a sigh.

"But what?" Ciji prompted.

"I think I really want him. Like...*want him* want him. Earlier today, when he was over here and we were in the midst of digging through the archival wreckage of our friendship, all I could think about was having him. In *that* way."

"Well, I suggest that you calm your little puss down... unless a mutually satisfactory, sex-only agreement is what the two of you decide upon. Coz don't get me wrong, that's always a vibe too. If that does end up being the case, I got some brand new, still in the packaging items that'll help you to really turn him out. But I... I dunno, not to sound all sappy, but I just don't get that vibe when I see him looking at you when he thinks no one else is looking. That man's feelings for you run *deep* deep, friend. So if you're not there... I can't tell you what to do, obviously because autonomy, but what I can say is taking your time never hurt nobody. Take a couple days to think on it. Then, when you make the right decision for you and him moving forward, you all can have the necessary conversation to move ahead however you see fit."

"Logically I know you're right, but you also have plied me with enough tequila tonight that's making me wanna say fuck logic," I groaned, then giggled.

"Well then I guess it's my responsibility to cock block until you pass out so I won't allow you to do something that you could live to regret on my watch. And in that case," Ciji said, pulling out her phone with flourish, "You got a taste for something in particular or are we gonna play takeout roulette?"

"You don't have a hot date to tie up that man of yours tonight?" I teased.

Ciji shook her head with a knowing grin. "Nah, he's on a SOS call not dissimilar to mine as a matter of fact."

Instead of taking the bait of that comment, I told her that I had a hankering for some Thai food and we commenced ordering takeout, drinking ourselves silly until it arrived, and then gorging on it once it was in my house. Intermittently, I wondered what Tony and Billy were talking about. And if he was thinking about me in any way. The overwhelming urge to see him stirred within me a little too deeply to take too much more time away, so instead of listening to the wise counsel of my good girlfriend, I found myself scrolling the email with contact information for everyone involved with Megamansion Makeover until I'd found Tony's number. Initially I told myself that I was just going to save the contact in my phone so that when I was ready to have another conversation with him, it would be at the ready. And then I poured myself the last of the trendy tequila that Ciji had brought over. And when I should have been going to bed, I scrolled through my phone until finding that newly installed contact and typing out a four word message. My finger hovered between the send and backspace buttons and before I lost the courage, I finally pressed send.

Wayland

Those were the words I saw splayed against my screen when I'd picked up my vibrating phone from a number I didn't recognize. The phone buzzed again with an additional message.

I hadn't needed her to tell me, I just intrinsically *knew*. But seeing those words instantly transported me back to when I was on the sending end of a very similar message to her a few years back. I'd been steamed when I'd sent the text, newly informed that my so-called best friend had been working to sabotage my relationship for what, at the time, had seemed like her own personal diversion.

Crissa had shown up to my house with a sheaf of papers, printouts of alleged back and forth conversations that she'd been having with KK intermittently over the past few months. Texts that could be construed as thinly veiled threats in some instances, which was the most incredulous part of the whole shit. At the end of the conversation with my girl, she'd given me an ultimatum—it was her or KK. After poring over the evidence, my choice was abundantly clear, I needed to sever ties with KK in order to keep who I'd thought was the love of my life in my life. So, I sent KK that text, inviting her to my place.

Since we were merely friends, she hadn't really seen anything ominous about it. She'd entered my place with her usually sunny smile and a pat to my shoulder as she passed me in the doorway. That smile quickly transformed into a look of confusion once she'd taken in my stormy countenance.

"What the fuck is wrong with you?" was how I'd started the conversation before she'd barely settled onto my couch.

Kalise's brow furrowed in confusion at my anger. "Tony, what are you..."

"These," I said, picking up the sheaf of papers from the coffee table in front of the couch and thrusting them in her direction. "What the fuck are these?"

Her eyes cast downward, she briefly scanned the screenshots before turning her gaze back to me, the heat of anger shining furiously from it now.

"I don't know, but I have a feeling you're going to tell me," Kalise replied coolly.

"Fuck all that, KK," I grumbled, "What are you on? Why would you do this? What do you stand to gain from trying to torpedo my life, huh?"

"You clearly have it all figured out, Tony," she replied a little too calmly, with a shrug, which just infuriated me further.

"And what the fuck is that supposed to mean?"

"It means that no matter what I say at this moment, you've clearly been fed a narrative that isn't sensical in any way. But, instead of actually stepping back and trying to see things clearly, you're choosing to just go along with what you've been fed."

"I didn't have to be fed shit, Kalise. It's all right there in black and white. 'He'll do whatever I say if I just snap my fingers.' 'You're just a temporary distraction.' 'Tony will never give you what you need because it all belongs to me.' So what, I'm your puppet or minion? Only here to submit to your needs?"

"Listen to what you're saying and tell me how that even sounds remotely like anything I would say. First of all, I don't talk like a bitch who didn't make it past the first audition for Love and Hip Hop Schenectady, for one. Secondly, when have I ever inserted

myself into anything with you and whoever your flavor of the month is, Tony?" she said, standing from the couch and walking right up on me. "It's not my style and never has been."

"Crissa isn't a flavor of the month, she's my future. Something you know nothing about since you barely wanna let a nigga get close enough to you to actually stick around because you're too scared of losing him." Kalise gasped and turned me to with a stricken look on her face that I ignored in favor of continuing my rant. "At first, I thought that maybe she was just a little jealous or had somehow misunderstood the bond that I shared with you, but reading all of this shit you've been sending her, for the past six fucking months, Kalise? I realize that I'm the one who had the shit wrong all this time."

"So, you're really just about to take her word at face value, huh? Off some bullshit?" she asked, throwing the papers in my direction.

"Bullshit or not, it's there as plain as day, KK. I don't really know what your angle is here but I can't keep somebody around me who is moving shaky like you are."

"And I don't have to maintain a friendship with someone who would believe a lie that was manufactured for them instead of really listening to what I'm saying is the truth."

And with those words she'd walked out of my place, never looking back.

Shortly thereafter my father had caught wind of the situation that'd unfolded between us and read me my rights immediately. He'd called me every version of stupid for blindly accepting Crissa's "truths" with the tenured history that Kalise and I had shared. At first I'd tried bucking back, but when I drilled down to the real reason why I'd been so quick to believe Crissa and what had truly made me upset about the whole situation it was easy to see that I was in the wrong. Unfortunately I'd realized that shit too little too late. It was wild that I even had this second chance with KK now considering the wild shit I'd said to her the day of that blow up. Hell, maybe after she'd had a bit of time to think about it a bit further, she wasn't going to grant me that second chance, but instead was using this opportunity to tell me that maybe we should just leave things where they've been. I hoped like hell that option wasn't how things would shake out.

"Ay, you finna cry yourself to sleep on my couch or what?" my brother asked as he walked back into the room with a couple more brews.

I'd been at his place since I'd skated out on KK earlier. I'd been embarrassed considering that I'd vowed to myself to let things with our reconciliation to happen naturally, then was just straight up unable to contain myself the minute she'd given me an inch. I came here to lick my wounds until I could figure out how to move forward.

"Fuck you, bruh," I shot back, laughing as I extended a hand to catch the beer he'd lobbed in my direction.

"I'm just saying, you been over here sighing like you're the lead in a fucking WB teen drama. When you need to just nut up and go *back* to her house and talk to that damn woman."

"You say that shit like it's a simple task," I replied.

"Because it is. Let's start with what we know. For starters, you know how stubborn KK is. So if she was still harboring any true resentment toward you and your asinine behavior from what...five, six years ago, then there was no way in hell she would have even looked in your direction, let alone give you the opportunity to be all up in her air space like you were the other night... and earlier today."

"Chill out on me."

"I'm just saying. If steam pressed was a person, nigga it woulda been you."

"You're enjoying this a little too much, my brother."

He offered me a shrug before breaking into a grin. "It's true, I am. But you finna take it because you came here for a reason."

"Only 'cause Daddy ain't answer his phone."

"Yeah aight. Never mind. Good luck getting the girl, bro. Matter of fact, lemme text Ciji and throw salt in your game instead."

"You're too late," I said with a smug grin as I held up my phone. "KK already reached out."

"Then why in the hell are you still here?"

"Because all she said was 'we need to talk'. Not exactly in a hurry to find out what exactly there is for us to talk about."

"Oh you shook for real. Aw shit, let me find out that Granny been right this whole time," Will crowed.

I don't know why that boy keep pussyfootin' 'round like that girl ain't his destiny unless he scared.

Those words were a common refrain we'd heard from my grandmother's lips over the years. I could damn near hear her amused tone sounding off in my ears now as soon as Billy had invoked her. She had always been the most vocal out of everyone who'd speculated over the years that the KK and I were destined to be more than "just friends". And I knew that she would likely get a kick out of my current predicament. Because the time had come for me to stop trying to deny what, in her mind, had always been an inevitability.

And I was more scared than a motherfucker.

"Why are you acting like this is news to you?" I asked my brother. As much as I tried to talk around it, he knew the depth of my feelings for Kalise, even if I'd never expressed them aloud. The connection between the two of us was why I'd immediately known what had him so bothered about his current lady before he got over himself and submitted to his destiny.

"Because despite knowing that your ass has been in love with that girl ever since you snuck out of the house and found her in our tree fort, I thought you'd cling to the stubborn notion of not letting that love lead the damn way until your dying days. Which would honestly just be plain stupidity. Actually, that's on brand for you. Because no matter how many times Daddy hammered the virtue of always trusting your gut into us over and over again, your ass always bucked the trend. Went against the grain because you never quite felt grounded in actually making decisions of your own volition."

"When the fuck did you become Iyanla in this bitch?"

"The minute I realized that you keep operating to your detriment. I love you, bro. Sincerely. More than just about anybody else on this earth, but if I've learned nothing in the time that I've shared with Ciji it's that trying to deny what's divinely ordered only leads to complication after complication. You have a choice here to choose simplicity, but the more you dodge it..."

"Complication," I finished, sighing as I shook my head. "I hear you, bruh, but..."

"No buts," Will said, holding up a hand. "Go pull up on that woman. Leaving her on read ain't the move, man."

I looked down at my phone, those four little words seeming to pop off the screen with an ominous glow. Until I finally tapped out a few words in reply.

On my way.

After dapping up Will and teasing Ciji when she walked up the steps to his place as I descended them, I was in my car and driving toward KK's place.

No wonder he was in such a hurry for me to leave, I thought as I shifted into gear.

By the time I'd pulled up to KK's, I'd come up with too many damn hypothetical scenarios for what exactly this talk she wanted us to have would include. I moved from the car to her front stoop at a snail's pace, convinced that what she had to say was something that I didn't want to hear. I pressed her doorbell and waited for her to answer. After a couple minutes had passed, I found myself pressing it again, growing more agitated when again more minutes passed without her coming to the door. I pulled out my phone, navigating to our text thread, calling the number and feeling like a supreme asshole when she answered with a sleep-addled, "Hello?"

"Hey, it's me. I'm outside but if now isn't..." I started but she quickly interrupted with a hurried, "No, hold on. Don't leave." I could hear rustling as she shuffled toward the front door, opening it shortly thereafter. I couldn't help but grin at how, despite her slumber-rumpled hair and heavy eyes she was still so fucking pretty.

"So–ooh," she said, then yawned. "Oh my god, I'm so sorry. Ciji and that damn tequila."

"If you want me to come back later, I can."

"No," she responded, instantly, her hand darting out to stop me from completing the turn to walk back to my car that I was halfway through as the words left my mouth. "Come in."

Her fingers tightened around my wrist and she urged me into her home and onward toward the living room. When we were in range, she flopped back onto her couch, snuggling under a blanket and looking at me expectantly. I sat down, kinda warily, simply because I wasn't quite sure what this was.

"You want anything? Something to drink? Eat?"

I shook my head. "I'm good, KK."

We sat for a few moments in silence before she spoke up again.

"Why did you never say anything?" she finally said as the silence stretched uncomfortably.

"About?" I asked, playing dumb.

"Don't do that, Tony. You know what I'm talking about."

"I thought it was a fool's errand. I'd never gotten any vibe that you would be open to me even bringing the subject up. Especially since you'd said so many times, 'uh uhn, this ain't that', whenever anyone would bring up the fact that our closeness perhaps was more than platonic."

She gave me a soft grin as I mimicked her voice. "You wanna know something?"

"Anything," I replied immediately. "Everything."

"I'm *so* nervous right now," she whispered, nearly inaudible, as she lowered her eyes and played with the edge of the blanket that covered her lap.

I moved in closer. "Why?"

She shrugged. "I don't know this just...it feels like a *moment*. One that I am not prepared for."

"I need you to say more things."

"I don't wanna say the wrong things and fuck this up," she said with a humorless chuckle. "I... we... what do you want from me, Tony?"

I let out a low chuckle. "Nothing more than you're willing to give, KK. I laid all my shit bare earlier, despite it being the absolute last thing I wanted to do. Because I wasn't about to let another twenty damn years pass by before I told you how I felt, for real. I've denied the fact that I've been in love with you well before I even knew what the fuck being in love really was, Kalise. I fully recognize that laying this out has the possibility of alienating you, but something deep down in me tells me that even if it's not where you are today, you could get there with me. Because I know I mean as much to you as you do to me and..."

She stopped my rant by leaning forward and

softly pressing her lips to mine, shocking the hell out of me. I quickly recovered though, moving my hand to cup her chin and increase the pressure of our conjoined lips before sliding my tongue along the seam of her lips. She easily acquiesced, opening her mouth and inviting my tongue to tangle with hers. Slowly, reluctantly, I pulled back after a few moments, waited for her to open her eyes and connect her gaze to mine.

"We've wasted so much time," she said after a few moments of us just staring at one another passed.

"Good thing we've got the rest of our lives to make up for that, huh?" I said, something that must've shocked her if the gasp she gave at my utterance was any indication.

"Tony, I..." she started, but I quickly shushed her with a finger to her lips.

"Chill. There's no rush, baby. I'm willing to work our way through this transition however slowly you need. Give us both the opportunity to figure all of this out. No matter how badly I want to just flip the switch, run outside and yell at the top of my lungs that you're mine right now, my daddy ain't raise no fool. I want to take my time with this because I don't want our connection to end up being a casualty in a needless war because we moved too fast from beefin' to... wherever we are right now. But know this, I'm about to enjoy every moment of this journey, savor every goddamn minute of what I've waited entirely too long to have."

"And what's that?" she asked breathlessly.

"*You,*" I responded honestly before lowering my head and capturing her sweet lips once again.

Kalise

After pulling back from the kiss he'd laid on me that felt like he was trying to consume me whole, Wayland sat back against the fluffy pillows of my couch, lower lip pulled between his teeth as he just stared unabashedly. Under his gaze, I felt stripped bare, as if he could see though any sort of facade I would dare attempt to put in place. It was unnerving and thrilling all at the same time.

"Can I ask you something?" I said after the silence stretched.

"Anything. Everything."

"So I know we agreed to slow roll our way into figuring out this progression of our relationship, but... will you stay?"

"Of course," he replied easily. "If that's what you want."

"It is. I just..." I trailed off not knowing exactly how to express the need that I felt deep within to just have him within arm's reach for tonight. Not even on some let me finesse my way into seeing what that dick do type of time, but his presence, in just this short amount of time, was deeply satisfying. Hell even when we were at odds, there was just something about being in this man's presence that settled my restless spirit. I'd been having fitful rest even since I'd moved back home, but intrinsically I knew that if he remained and I was in his arms as I drifted, then tonight's battle would be less hard fought. He'd always had that effect on me from when he'd talked me out of trying to become a Black Boxcar kid way back in the day. I hadn't had the language to properly categorize it then, but now I knew it was because for me he had always been the human manifestation of a safe space.

"You just?" he prompted.

I shook my head to clear the reservation that had halted my tongue.

"I didn't want to make things weird."

"One thing's for certain," he said, moving in closer to speak directly into my ear. "The only weird thing is just how much we played until finally getting to this point." He pressed a light kiss to my neck just below my earlobe before standing and urging me to my feet. "C'mon, let's get you to bed."

We were halfway toward my bedroom before he

stopped short. "Hold on, let me run to the car real quick and see if I got a change of clothes in my gym bag. I know how weird your ass used to be about folks being on your bed in their street clothes and I'd bet anything that with increased age that's gotten worse."

"Shut up," I whined, playfully shoving him.

"I'll take that as a yes. Gon' head and get into your little pre-bedtime routine. I'll be back before you've reached the fiftieth step."

I rolled my eyes as he leaned down to peck my lips softly then turned and made his way outside.

It was weird because despite the fact that we'd been estranged for these years he still knew *me*. Because it hadn't popped into my brain previously, but I knew as soon as I saw my bed I would have been giving him a side eye about hopping into it wearing the tee and sweats he'd come from outdoors with. I went straight into my ensuite bathroom and began my wind down routine, yet another thing about me that hadn't changed in the years since Tony and I were thick as thieves. This was something I'd actually gotten from my stepmother, Alma, the importance of leaving the day behind before I stepped into bed. My routine was fairly simple, but Tony had always teased me about the rigidity I maintained about sticking to it. Back in the day he'd hated routines almost as much as Mrs. Thomas's college algebra class, so his teasing was to be expected.

I was brushing my teeth, bobbing my head along to the soft music that played from my phone when he stuck his head into the bathroom, already changed into basketball shorts and a tee. He must've used my guest bedroom to do a quick change.

"You got a spare one of those?" he asked, gesturing toward the toothbrush.

Since my mouth was otherwise occupied, I lifted my chin and canted it in the direction of the small utility closet that was just outside of my bathroom that held my spare linens, towels, and other accoutrements needed for any hygienic needs. When he rejoined me and we stood elbow to elbow brushing our teeth, there was a fluttery feeling in my stomach. We'd certainly been in this position before, having shared community spaces on various trips we'd taken with friends back in the day, but this felt different. Especially once I'd finished brushing my teeth and moved on to doing my nightly skincare routine and he remained in the bathroom, braced against the door frame just taking me in.

"What?" I asked.

"Nothing, just admiring the view," he replied smoothly and I rolled my eyes to mask the complete thrill of excitement that blazed through my body from the simple compliment.

Once I'd completed my whole routine and we argued about him insisting on sleeping on my side of the bed because of some asinine "first line of defense" rule he had in his head, we finally settled into my bed, side by side, but not quite touching. Tony lay on his back, eyes closed, breathing slowly evening out as I mimicked his positioning before turning onto my side. I guess presenting my back to him was the cue he'd needed to follow in the direction I now faced and settle right behind me, his arm loosely draping across my waist.

"This is okay, yeah?" he said, the gruff sound of his voice damn near making me whimper.

Instead of a vocal reply, I readjusted, pushing myself further into the defined planes of his form and pulling that arm of his more snugly about me. As he burrowed his face into my neck from behind, I could feel his mouth hike up into a smile before he whispered, "Sweet dreams, KK."

"Ni-night, Tony," I murmured back.

The comfort of his embrace was stronger than melatonin as I hadn't even recalled falling asleep. Usually I tossed and turned for sometimes up to ninety minutes before my brain finally settled and the sandman was ushered in. Last night, however, my mind was blissfully settled.

If anyone had told me two weeks ago that I would be waking up deeply ensconced between Wayland Anthony Preston's arms with one leg thrown over his hip as I pressed my sweet spot into the prominent bulge between his thighs, I would have called you everything but a child of God. Hell, if you'd told me the same three days ago, my reaction may have held a little less bite, but would have been in the same ballpark. But as I awakened this morning and came to the realization that I was not alone in my bed and waking up in the arms of my former yet recently reacquainted best friend, it hadn't felt weird at all.

It felt a little *too* comfortable if I was keeping myself honest.

A realization that made me try to wrest from his grip and take a moment to myself.

The man in question, however, wasn't trying to let that happen as his hand on my waist tightened and he pulled me more into his body, placing soft kisses along my neck.

"Good morning," he murmured into my skin and I shivered at the surge of passion the simple contact had unleashed within me.

I knew last night that we'd decided to take it slow, but those lingering kisses paired with his wandering hands gently caressing my thighs as his dick made its presence known even further between my thighs made me throw caution to the wind. Using a bit of momentum, I rolled us over so that I was straddling his waist and now looking down at him. He stared up at me with sleep-heavy lids, a brow raised as if he was waiting on me to make my move. I cupped his face, sliding my fingers along the dusting of hair on his cheeks and chin before leaning down and pressing a closed-mouth kiss to his lips. As much as I wanted to deepen that contact, I knew my breath —and his—was likely trash as fuck this morning, but I didn't let that stop me from taking things further. I nibbled my way from his lips to his ear whispering, "I want you so fucking bad right now."

"I thought we were taking it slow," he teased as he moved his hands from my waist to my ass, gripping it with intensity, deepening the contact that the slow undulations of my hips into his made between his ever-growing bulge and my embarrassingly wet pussy.

I pulled back, removing the tank top that I wore with nothing beneath it and his eyes were laser-focused on my breasts that grew heavier under his perusal, my protruding nipples beading as his gaze seared them. He quickly got the hint, shifting us so that I was now on my back again and he lowered his mouth to feast on my body. Slowly making his way downward, starting at my collarbone, licking and nipping at it then kissing a path to the center of my chest while his hands ran up my body to both settle on the undersides of my breasts, holding them together as he lowered his face into them and let out a growl. When he took one of my nipples into his mouth and worried it with his teeth as he pinched and rubbed the other, I writhed beneath him, moaning at the sensations evoked. My breasts had always been highly sensitive, something he must've quickly picked up on as he teased and manipulated them to the point of me panting his name, begging for release. His fingers stayed at my nipples, alternately flicking and pinching at them, as his mouth traveled further south. His lingering, lip-smacking kisses along my torso had my abdomen concave the further he sank. I rested my hands atop his head, gently pushing him toward a destination that he was, in my opinion, taking far too long to get to.

"Eager, are we, baby? I'ma get there," he crooned against my skin, the rush of the air leaving his mouth as he spoke making me break out into goose pimples.

"Tony, please," I moaned as he nosed my navel before removing my sleep shorts completely and diving face first between my legs.

The first swipe of his tongue against my pussy was both welcomed relief and overwhelming bliss. His tongue flickered against my clit as he slid two fingers deep into my opening, gliding them in a rhythm that had me rotating my hips to match.

"I knew your pussy would taste this sweet," he murmured before burying his face so deeply between my legs I momentarily worried for his ability to breathe. That worry was quickly allayed by the sounds he made as he devoured me. I felt every exhalation and inhalation against my most sensitive places as he continuously praised the look, touch, taste, and feel of my pussy. Before long I was cumming with an extra gush of wetness and a sharp cry as my back arched from the bed.

"Tooooooo-neeeeeeee," I keened, breaking those two syllables into what sounded like a damned battle cry as he ate me through my orgasm and then some.

I was splayed on the bed, feeling absolutely boneless when he finally came up from between my legs, bringing his mouth to mine to share the taste of my pussy with me. Greedily, I welcomed his tongue in my mouth as I savored the unique flavor created by our natural essences combined. After a few moments, he released me from the kiss, removing his clothing and coming back to rejoin me in the bed. Taking his in dick without the barrier of shorts holding it back gave me my second wind as I sat up, immediately grabbing it with one hand and stroking it.

"Shit, KK," he grunted and I grinned like a proud demon at just my touch making him a little crazy.

"Is this all for me?" I asked teasingly.

"Absolutely, babe. To do whatever you want with it *except* playing," he gritted out as I quickened my strokes.

"In that case," I said as I straddled his thighs, my warm, wet pussy hovering just above the mushroomed tip of his dick, "I guess I better get to work huh?"

We shared a moan as I sank down onto him slowly, taking my time once I was fully seated before

I started moving. His hands instantly went to my ass as I bounced up and down on his shaft, loving the way he felt as he filled me up.

"You feel so *good*," I moaned as I increased my speed.

His hands clamped on my waist, trying to control my movements as he returned, "Shiiiiit, that's all you, baby. You ridin' the fuck out this dick. You gon cum for me on this dick?"

"Mmmmmmm," I moaned, swatting at his hands while maintaining my rhythm.

He caught the hint, moving his hands to be of use elsewhere as he cupped my titties again, pulling them toward his mouth. As he suckled one nipple deep into his mouth, I shifted my positioning, moving from riding him with my knees braced on the mattress to balancing on the balls of my feet as I worked my way up and down, my ass making contact with his thighs on each of my downstrokes. That shift in positioning also opened me up a bit wider and he took advantage of the access to my clit, sliding a hand from my breasts down my stomach, pinching the sensitive button between his thumb and fore-finger as he shifted them back and forth. My stomach began to quake as I was overcome with sensation, damn near catapulting over the edge into orgasm once again.

"I'm... I'm... about to cummmmmmmm," I whined

as my legs tremored, then gave out and I collapsed onto him.

Tony kept the party going, hands at my waist as he reversed our positions and pummeled into me mercilessly, pulling my thighs around his waist as I was yeeted into the sensual abyss, my entire being tingling as my orgasm rushed over me. He harshly grunted "fuck" and slowed his movements as he emptied his seed into me before collapsing his full body weight onto me. It was only briefly before he removed himself, but I would have gladly stayed trapped beneath his mass because it felt just that good. I wasn't sure how much time passed before he got up and returned with a warm, soapy towel to clean up the mess we'd made between my legs, but I was barely with him, completely drained from the energy that this fuck had expended and right back into dreamland before he'd even thrown the towel on my bedside table.

A few hours later, I awakened again to our beautifully nude bodies entangled in one another's. Memories of the way he'd taken my body on a thrilling erotic ride just hours ago had me feeling better than good and I was loath to leave this space, but the dire need to relieve my bladder won out over me lingering. Plus, I looked over at the clock, peeped the time, and knew I needed to get my day going. I hadn't gotten too far before I felt the strong grip of his hand resting at my waist. The immediate rush of warmth that traveled through my body had me shaking my head to get it back in the game.

"Where are you going?" he murmured, pulling my body back into his.

"I've gotta get up and help Alma bring my dad home."

That night my dad went into the hospital, and they ran every test possible in order to rule things out, the doctor had seen a few things on his scans that were concerning. As such, they'd kept him in the hospital a couple more days, just to make sure everything was on the up and up once they finally let him come home. I'd told Alma that I would meet her at the hospital and bring them home to make sure my dad was good and settled. I knew that caring for him with his declining health wasn't easy on her, so I made myself accessible and expendable whenever she needed me. Something I could tell she greatly appreciated because despite loving my daddy's dirty draws, we all needed a break from the heaviness of life sometimes.

Way loosened his grip and let me scoot out of bed. He swung his legs over the side and asked, "How's the old man?"

"Doing well enough that they don't need to keep him monitored around the clock for any longer. Though, his worrisome ass is about to come home and wreak havoc on me and Alma now," I replied, making my way into the bathroom.

"And the both of y'all are gonna love every minute. Hell, doting on Big Kenny is one of your favorite pastimes," Wayland yelled through the closed door.

I grinned at his assessment. He was right. My daddy had done so much for me, sacrificed a lot to make sure that I was able to live the best life possible, so it truly wasn't a thing for me to give that energy right back now that I was in adulthood. He and Alma both deserved the world and I'd do everything in my power to give it to them. I finished up in the bathroom and returned to my room with Way still standing on the side of the bed he'd slept on, as he stretched his hands over his head. Watching the sinewy muscles of his body as he stretched had me biting down on my lip so I wouldn't moan aloud. *Goddamn he was so fine.*

"After that though, what you got going on?" Tony pressed.

"Daaaaang," I replied teasingly, "Let the man get up in your guts one time and he wanna take up all of your time. I thought we were slow rolling, sir."

"Look at you fronting like you don't wish we could get back up in this bed and lay up all day. Ol' cuddle bunny headass," he said, rounding the bed and slinging his arms low around my waist. I immediately relaxed into his embrace, staying purposefully quiet because he was right. I was lowkey wishing I could luxuriate in this time of us being together before everyone else knew there was an "us together" to be concerned about. "What time are you meeting Alma? You got enough time for me to treat you to breakfast?"

On cue, my stomach sounded off with a growl that would have put a lion's roar to shame. I hung my head, lowkey embarrassed.

"I'll take that as a yes," he teased.

"Yes, I absolutely do have time for that. What you cooking me?"

"It's groceries in here?"

"You know, if you're gonna keep giving me shit, I might have to rethink this whole 'give a relationship with Tony a shot' thing we've got going on here," I grumbled.

"Don't be like that, baby. You know it's all in fun," he replied before burying his face in my neck and pressing a series of soft kisses in a spot that he shouldn't have known was *the* spot this quickly, so I couldn't complain any further. "I need to go to the crib, shit shower shave and all that, but I'll be back here in about an hour to take you wherever you wanna go for breakfast. How's that work?"

"Sounds like a plan."

"Bet it up, then," he said, releasing me from his embrace and moving toward the items he'd stowed on the recliner in the corner of my room that I hadn't even noticed last night. Quickly donning the shorts and tee he'd slept in, his socks, and sneakers, he looked up at me and said, "Come walk me out and lock the door behind me?"

With a nod I grabbed my robe off the hook on the back of my door, draped myself in it, and followed him to my front door, bracing in the frame when instead of just continuing through and walking down my steps he turned back to face me. He placed a hand at my chin and stared for a few seconds, wordlessly while biting down on his lip before he shook his head as he bent down to press a sweet kiss to my temple.

"Okay this is cuuuuuute," I heard trilled from across the way. "Morning, y'all!"

I turned to see Ciji getting out of her car and heading up to her doorway. Tony gave her a head nod of acknowledgement before he took his leave and instead of heading to her place, she made a beeline straight over to mine. I couldn't close the door quick enough and she snuck right on in.

"Soooooo?" Ciji prodded.

"You're out early," I replied.

She rolled her eyes and scrunched up her face at me. "Uh uhn, don't even. Especially since last I'd thought you were taking some time to try and figure out if you even wanted to go there with him."

"And that time passed a little quicker than antici-pated," I replied back, grinning mischievously.

"I seeeeeee," she teased, wriggling her brows. "Shut me right on up because you clearly didn't need any time. You're over here shining like freshly polished silver. That man put you to sleep and woke you up early, ain't it?"

"You get on my nerves," I said, laughing. "We honestly just talked things out and...yeah."

"That's a start!" Ciji said, clapping her hands together. "Oh this is about to be fun. We can double date, do game nights and shit, and..."

I held up a hand, halting the locomotive that was her brain already chugging along with ideas of all of us being some sort of fearsome foursome or something. "We're slow rolling, Ceej. Taking our time. So maybe relax on all of that stuff you were talking about just now."

"You are just so... you know what. I'm not gonna say that. But ooh I can't wait to be able to say 'I told you so' to your ass in the near future. Because I just have a feeling."

"Yeah yeah. Get your behind out of here, I gotta get showered and dressed before Tony gets back so we can get to breakfast before I go pick up my dad and Alma."

"How is everything on that front?" Ciji asked, clear concern lacing her tone.

"We're on the right path. Dad's gotta do some shit with cleaning up his diet and getting some daily movement in, but other than that, he'll be alright, I think. He's been worrying the hell out of those people at the hospital though so I know they'll be glad to finally discharge him."

"Good, I'm so glad to hear that. All right, girl. I'll get out of your hair so you can get cute for your man," Ciji said.

"He saw this when he woke up, the mystery is already gone," I deadpanned and Ciji rolled her eyes.

"Not the bitch who looks like a fresh faced undergrad talkin' this mess. Bye, girl."

She left my house and I set about getting ready so I'd just need to slip on my shoes and walk out of the door once Tony returned. While trying to decide what to wear, I vacillated between going full-on glam or just giving my normal energy. Eventually I settled somewhere in the middle. Alma had called and my dad's doc was supposed to be to see him around noon and then he'd be discharged shortly after, so I had more than enough time to get breakfast, come back home, and make my way to the hospital.

I also checked in with the manager at our retail store to make sure everything was still rolling smoothly. She was a recent hire, the only candidate who'd met the stringent requirements I'd held for anyone that I would be turning that part of the business over toward. The group out at the farm was ruled by Chap, one of my dad's mentees, and he kept them together and running like a well-oiled machine. He'd welcomed the increased responsibility that came with my return and my father's stepping back in the day to day of Worthington Farms and the nursery.

It had taken a bit, but now that I'd finally gotten our business out of disarray, I was excited for the growth opportunities. Doing Megamansion Makeover would definitely go a long way in ensuring that the business stayed trending in the black. Lowkey, Rachel had been hinting at wanting to use plants, trees, and shrubs from Worthington across the network and truthfully? If the money was right and the needs weren't beyond what we could afford to add to workflow and still produce naturally, I'd be all for it. I knew that the Preston Brothers had been trying to convince Daddy to do it for years and he'd resisted, for reasons I was quite certain had to do more with interpersonal drama than actual business. Despite Daddy Preston and my dad being thick as thieves, he had still felt some kind of way about Wayland. I giggled, thinking about how I'd have to tell my dad that he needed to build a bridge and get over that because Tony and I were definitely a thing now.

Wayland

After spending the night with and subsequently having breakfast with Kalise, I was walking a little taller, swagger a little stronger. When I'd dropped KK back home so she could go retrieve her father from the hospital, we decided to play the rest of the day by ear because she didn't know how long she would be tied up with her folks. I was trying not to act too thirsty since I'd told her that we could slow roll this shit, but truthfully? I was more parched than a motherfucker and hoped like hell that getting her pops settled wouldn't take too long so I could be back in her presence sooner rather than later. I didn't have shit else to do so after a few hours had passed and I'd yet to hear back from KK I decided to slide by my pops' house and brag a lil bit about not only fixing things between me and KK, but also getting the damn girl.

Final-fucking-ly!

When I walked in through his back door I was surprised to see a woman with a face that looked kind of familiar sitting at the table while Daddy was filling up two bowls of soup. He turned around at the sound of the door opening and frowned when he saw me.

"Aw hell, what do you want?"

"Dang, Daddy! Is that any way to greet your favorite son in front of company? Sorry he's so rude, ma'am," I said to the woman who just tittered at our back and forth.

"Laura ain't no damn company, she damn near family, boy. You don't remember Alma's sister?"

While that did explain the slight twinge of famil-iarity I'd had upon seeing her face, I couldn't say that I quite remembered her. But I knew that if I said I hadn't, I'd be taken on a trip down memory lane that would last far too long until something triggered a memory.

"Ah yes, how could I forget a face as beautiful as this one? How you been, Ms. Laura?" I said charm-ingly, going over to embrace her briefly.

"Just fine, baby. Had to come up here and see about my sister since I could just tell that she wasn't telling me the whole truth about everything going on with Kenny. Called myself popping up on them only for nobody to be home. Thank goodness Harold saw me and filled me in a little bit. Now I'm just hanging over here 'til they make it in," she rambled.

I just nodded with a smile as she went on until my dad brought the bowls toward the table and then she tucked into eating like it'd been forty days and forty nights since she'd had her last meal.

"You never said what you want, boy," my father questioned me between spoonfuls of his meal.

"I didn't want anything. Just came over to spend some quality time with my daddy. Is that a crime these days, sheesh?"

His gaze narrowed in on me like he was trying to figure something out before he gave me a large grin, nodding his head at me. "You figured your shit out, didn't you? This visit was a victory lap," he said with a laugh. "Well good on you, son. Took ya long enough."

I chuckled. "Aight, you got me, man. I did come over here to talk my shit, but I'ma let you and Miss Laura enjoy your lunch. Big Kenny and Miss Alma should be on the way pretty soon I think. Actually, Daddy, do you still have that spare key to their place? I wanna take a look at something before they get back."

When we were at breakfast, Kalise had mentioned that it was sometimes hard for her dad to be able to maneuver around the house since he had started relying on the use of the walker more and more over the cane he'd previously favored. I wanted to take a look at the bones of the structure to see if we could do a minimally intrusive remodel that'd allow for ease of access for Big Kenny. It hadn't been something that I'd shared with KK at the time, but my wheels had definitely begun turning about it.

"On the hook up front next to my other keys," my father replied.

I grabbed them and headed over to the Worthingtons. It'd been a while since I'd been inside of this house and as soon as I crossed the threshold of the front door a deluge of memories washed over me like waves on a shore. If we weren't at my house causing a ruckus, we were over here doing the same, much to Miss Alma's chagrin. Back then Big Kenny worked marathon days, splitting his time between being out at the farm and then, in later years, at their retail nursery location. As the door gaped open behind me I could almost hear Miss Alma yelling for me to not let all her good air conditioning out to cool the neighborhood. I shut the door and took a cursory walk around the first and second floors, immediately flooded with ways to make this place more accessible for Big Kenny once he was back home. I took a few pics and jotted down a few things in my notes app to discuss with KK later. I knew she might balk at it because it would be yet another expense for her parents, but if he had another episode or worse stroke, a fully accessible floor plan would go a long way to aiding in his recovery efforts.

"Wayland!" I heard my father yelling from downstairs so I jogged down to see what was going on.

"What's up, Daddy?" I said once I was back on the ground floor.

"Alma called. Kenny done had another episode. We're about to ride on up there now," he said, turning to leave.

"I'ma lock up and I'm right behind y'all," I replied. As soon as I got behind the wheel of my car I knew that I'd likely beat them there because my first thoughts went to KK and how she was handling herself. Daddy hadn't said much about Big Kenny's condition, but I'd assume that it wasn't horrible considering how calm he'd been. I needed to get to her quickly and make sure that she knew that I was here for her to lean on.

Once I'd parked and checked in with reception at the hospital I was on the elevator on my way up to Big Kenny's room. I took a few deep breaths, trying to steel myself for what I might see. I didn't like hospitals. Hadn't since I was a kid and had to get my tonsils taken out. Hadn't helped that this was the same hospital in which my grandmother had taken her last breath thanks to cancer ravaging her body. I needed to put all of those feelings aside for the time being so that I could make sure that Kalise was good. The last thing she needed was me crumbling while she was trying to figure out life for them going forward since her father's health was taking this steep decline. When I got to the room, Big Kenny was asleep and Miss Alma was at his bedside. I crept in quietly, going over to give her a quick hug and kiss, before saying, "How you holdin' up, Miss Alma?"

She looked up at me and squinted for a second before saying, "Oh I'm making it, Wayland. It was a little scary there for a minute, but I think we'll be alright."

"Did KK leave?" I asked.

"Ladybug needed a minute. I think she said something about going to get some coffee," Miss Alma murmured.

"Alright, I'll go see if I can find her. My daddy and Miss Laura should be here soon," I offered.

"Oh lord, now who done told her worrisome ass to come up here!" Miss Alma grumbled.

Knowing that I needed to get out the jam instantaneously if that was her response to her sister's presence, I gave her another hug and said my goodbyes before that turned into a scene I didn't want to be a part of. I wandered down to the cafeteria of the hospital to see if I would find KK there. When I hadn't, I pulled out my phone and shot her a text. After a few minutes with no response, I went out to the parking lot to see if I saw her car still at the hospital. It was there—and empty—so I went back into the hospital again, wandering about until I thought a little deeper about where Kalise could possibly be. I doubled back past the cafeteria and through the atrium until I reached the secret garden that was hidden in the center of the hospital. There she sat on a stone bench in the middle of the space, with a spaced-out look on her face.

I went to her instantly, settling onto the bench next to her and pulling her into my arms as soon as I was seated. Lord only knows how long she'd been sitting there, but apparently my presence was her cue to allow that dam that had been holding her emotions back to give way because she immediately broke down into sobs in my embrace. I let her get it all out, rubbing her back and intermittently murmuring words of encouragement. I couldn't imagine how she was feeling, especially if she'd been here to actually see him have another episode.

When she was composed again, she pulled back and looked up at me. It just about broke me down to see the sheer pain and terror in her eyes. She opened her mouth to speak, but said nothing, instead swallowing hard and looking away from me for a second before reconnecting our gazes.

"How did you...?" she trailed off.

"I was out by my daddy's and Miss Alma had called to tell him what was going on with Big Kenny. He and Miss Laura should be pulling up soon."

"Auntie Laura is here?" Kalise asked.

"Yeah, she said she'd come into town to check on

Miss Alma since she felt like she wasn't being truthful with her."

Kalise harrumphed. "That's unsurprising."

"You wanna talk about it?" I asked.

She shook her head, but kept talking anyway. "That was the scariest moment of my life, I swear to God, Tony. We were getting him all settled to go and he was complaining about having to be transported down to the front in a wheelchair. One minute he was wisecracking and the next he was slurring his words sounding like the town drunk. Thank God that nurse was right there and she was a quick thinker because she immediately recognized the signs of a potential second stroke and sprang into action immediately to make sure it wasn't fatal."

"Fuck," I said, tightening my embrace around KK again, "I'm so sorry you had to witness that, baby."

"You wanna know the worst part? It was his own stubbornness that got him here. Apparently the doctor wasn't going to let him out today, something I didn't find out until after I got here today. He forced their hand to be released against medical advice and Alma sided with him. Now *clearly* these people have to know what they're doing in here but because his cantankerous behind wanted to be home, instead of letting them have a few more days to make sure that he was truly safe to come home, he'd put up such a big fuss that they finally agreed to let him go. Then this happens before he can even get in the damn wheelchair good enough. Now just imagine if this had happened at the house instead of here with trained medical professionals. Thankfully they were able to get him stabilized quickly, but that shit was harrowing, Tony. And Alma and her histrionics didn't help. While we were in the waiting area as they attended to him, I wanted to knock fire from her ass a smooth ten times. And I know she was just wildin' because she was worried, but I just didn't have it in me to be worried about her at that moment. I was too far in my own head about what had happened and what that meant for my dad's mortality, you know?"

"I'm so sorry you had to do that on your own, baby," I said, pressing a soft kiss to the top of her head. "Everything all good with Big Kenny now? I mean, he was knocked out when I was up there, so I'm hoping that's a good sign."

"Before I finally just left, we'd been waiting on the doctor to confirm if that was another TIA or a stroke this time. They gave him meds, got him stable, took him for another MRI, so I decided to take some time to breathe. I couldn't take Alma with her degree from Grey-Sloan Memorial University trying to tell me what she thought, so I told her I was going to get coffee and just left. I couldn't just sit there not knowing anything."

"Completely understandable, babe."

"God, this is just so... I don't need this shit right now, Tony. I just...I can't..." she trailed off as she started crying again. "I can't lose him. Now right now. Not like this."

"He's still here, baby," I murmured, trying to make her feel somewhat better. "And I bet this will be what will make his ass shape up so he can remain here for as long as possible. It's not his time yet, I promise."

"You can't promise something like that," she replied between sniffles.

"Aight, you may have me there," I replied soothingly. "But you gotta know that whatever I can do to make you feel better, to ease your mind, then I'm going to try my damn hardest to make it a reality. So even if I gotta go in there myself and scrub in on a surgery on Big Kenny's brain, I'm all in on making sure that he ain't going nowhere yet. Not like this, anyway. Hell, I didn't even get to..." I trailed off, wisely shutting myself up before I said something that would have sent KK running for the hills.

"You didn't get to what?" she asked. Apparently she had been listening more keenly than I'd thought.

"Convince him to finally sign the contract for Worthington to supply the show..." I replied, quickly.

Kalise leaned back, staring at me intently, like she was trying to figure something out before she huffed out, "Yeah okay," and giggled. "I would actually be the one who you'd have to convince since technically I'm in charge now."

"Oh that ain't no problem, now. I got ways of persuasion you ain't even seen yet, girl."

"Are you really creeping on me while I'm crying over my daddy? *Woooooow*, Tony. That's a new low."

I started stammering over my words before I felt her shoulders shaking and she looked up at me with a sly smirk.

"Sorry, you left me wide open for that one," she said contritely.

"Yeah yeah, your ass must be feeling better. You wanna go back up and see if they have any updates on your dad?"

She heaved a heavy sigh. "Not especially."

"Aight, then we can just kick it out here 'til you say you are then."

We sat in silence for a few moments more before she spoke up again. "You remember how hard I pushed for this?" She gestured to the space around us.

It hadn't been more than a year after she'd come to live near us that she'd come up with the idea of redoing and dedicating this garden space in honor of her mother. While her mother had been battling cancer, one of her favorite places to visit in the hospital where she received treatment had been an enclosed garden space similar to this one. KK had spent a lot of time with her mother in that garden and wanted to recreate something here that could possibly be as therapeutic to patients at our local hospital as that garden had been for her and her mother. It had taken burrowing through a lot of red tape, but her father had moved hell and high water to make sure his baby girl had the space to operate. I remembered being so impressed at just how much she knew about plants. I mean, yeah it was her family business, but KK had always been super knowledgeable about all aspects of botany. Many a day my eyes had glazed over as she went full-on plant nerd. I'd never stopped her from talking about them though because the way her eyes sparkled when she was in full nerd tilt was mesmerizing.

"I remember even more how you enlisted me and Billy's help for some of the installation of some of these plants," I said, chuckling.

"Oh please, y'all had fun. *We* had fun. I haven't been out here in so long. It still looks so good though."

I grabbed her hand, pulling her up from the bench where we were sitting and heading over to a small thicket of trees. "I wonder if it's still here," I said as my eyes searched the trunks of the four trees.

"Oh my god, I forgot about that! It's gotta be," she replied, instantly knowing what I was looking for as she traipsed in front of me and into the mulch surrounding the trees.

We'd carved our initials and the date into the

trunk of one of the trees at the completion of the project, just me and her though, Billy wasn't tryna do shit but leave at that point. We'd exceeded his manual labor threshold and he was over us at that point. But KK had been insistent that we leave our own mark somehow, beyond the bronzed plaque that indicated the garden had been renovated by Worthington in honor of her mother.

"Found it!" she said, a huge grin spreading over her face as I stepped next to her to see our janky ass attempting at carving. Neither of us could wield a knife worth a damn at that time so the letters were all shaky and jagged. But there they were KW + WP. We hadn't even been able to carve the entire date, only the month and day before we gave up the ghost.

"You wanna know something crazy?" I asked.

"What's that?" Kalise asked softly.

"This lowkey might have been where I first fell in love with you. Because even though that night I'd found you in our tree fort I knew I wanted to always try to make you feel better, it was after completing this project that I knew that whatever you'd ask of me whenever I would do it. Because the look in your eyes once the whole thing was unveiled and your mom's plaque was installed is literally one of my top ten personal best moments in life. Hell, top three even."

"Really?" she asked in a hushed, awe-filled tone.

I nodded before lowering my face to hers and

speaking right onto her lips before I captured them with mine. "Really. That night I told you, whatever you need I got you. And I meant that. Now we might have had a slight hiccup, but I'm glad we've managed to get back on track. And on that note, c'mon." I threaded my fingers through hers and pulled her toward the garden's exit. "Let's go see about Big Kenny."

Kalise

I should have been still worried about my father but the only thing I could think about was mounting this man that stood beside me and riding him until the cows came home. What a difference a few months made. As we rode the elevator back up to my father's room, he held my hand tightly, rubbing the top of it softly with his thumb. When the ding sounded that let us know we'd arrived at our destination, he let me precede him, but stopped me from taking more than a couple steps. I turned to him with a questioning look on my face.

"You good?" he asked, brows raised.

I nodded once. "Thanks to you, yes," I replied honestly.

The grin that covered his face instantaneously was infectious and I found myself returning it.

"Remember, no matter what they say is

happening with Big Kenny, I got you. I got y'all. However and whenever you need, aight?"

"Aight," I murmured before taking a deep breath and leading the way to my father's room.

We approached the door at the same time that his primary care doctor was strolling up, so this was perfect timing.

"Hey Doc Stein," I said.

"Kalise, good to see you again," he replied. "You're right on time, I was just about to go in and give your folks an update."

"Babe, I'll wait out here for you," Wayland said but I immediately shook my head.

"Come in, please?"

He nodded and squeezed my hand as we walked into the room. I'd expected to see Daddy Preston and my aunt Laura in the room with Alma when we entered, but it was just her and my dad, who was now awake. I took a seat in the bench style seating near the window across from Alma and Wayland settled in beside me. My dad looked over at us with a hint of surprise in his gaze, but didn't say anything.

"Good afternoon, Kenneth, Alma," Doctor Stein greeted, nodding his head at both of them as he spoke their names. "I wanted to give you all an update on Kenneth's condition, but first I need to just do a quick examination of him."

The rest of us remained quiet as he asked my dad a series of questions, then had him perform some very basic physical tasks. Seeing my daddy struggle to maintain control of the limbs on the left side of his body immediately had my eyes welling up, but I swallowed hard, willing myself not to cry yet again. My tears weren't going to solve anything, but it was quite jarring to see my father, the man I'd thought to be the strongest, who could withstand any sort of physical difficulty, being felled like this.

"The MRI that we did shortly after Kenneth's episode revealed that it was not another TIA, but a stroke that he suffered from today. Thankfully you all hadn't left here yet so we were able to administer the proper meds to ensure that it didn't turn fatal, but now we need to start having the conversations about how to progress forward. Unlike his previous incident, this one is a bit more impactful and unfortunately, it won't be a matter of just keeping him here to be monitored for a few days and then sending him home. We need to get Kenneth into an inpatient rehabilitation center for the next sixty days and we'll evaluate his progress to determine when he will be released to go home."

"Doc, I don't think—" Alma started and I immediately piped up to cut her off.

"This rehabilitation center, can you give us a few more details about it?" I asked.

"It's a hospital specifically dedicated to rehabilitation, so he'll be under the care of an entire team that will be focused on his recovery from this stroke.

Kenneth will be serviced by a team including a neurologist, dietician, case manager, various rehab therapists, and a psychologist to help him along as he works to get back to a space where it is healthy for him to be back home with you all. I'm intimately familiar with a lot of the staff at the rehab hospital and feel confident that he will receive the best standard of care to get him back on track. I know it's not ideal, being away from home for so long, but it is imperative to his recovery. You all will be able to visit him as often as you'd like during the hospital visitors hours and I am certain that the team there will also have a sit down with you both to outline the specifics of his rehabilitation care. Currently they're confirming that they have a room available for Kenneth. Once those details are ironed out, then we will discuss transport and all of that. Do you have any questions?"

I shook my head and cut my eyes to Alma to let her know that she didn't have any questions either. We needed to have a conversation about the two of them being realistic about my dad's health and what was needed to make sure he continued getting better and not regressing. Prior to moving back, I'd been under the impression that his health concerns were minor at best, but in the time I've been home I could see that Alma was just an accomplice in aiding his penchant to be lax when it came to caring for himself. I could tell that she thought she was doing what was best, standing by her man and all of that, but there came a time when in order to ensure someone was truly going to be alright that you may have to make them do things that they don't want to. And I was putting my foot down here. I did not want my dad to end up worse off because he was too damn stubborn to listen to astute medical advice and go through the proper rehabilitation.

"Not now, Doc, though I'm sure we'll have some going forward. Thank you so much."

Doc Stein smiled. "Of course, I'll let you all discuss things further. You can always have the nurses page me if there's something more you need from me."

Once he left the room, I spoke up immediately.

"I know that wasn't what either of you wanted to hear, but y'all have got to be realistic at this point," I started.

"You don't have to be disrespectful," Alma said.

"Disre—who have I disrespected?" I asked.

"Cutting me off in front of Doctor Stein for one. Steamrolling over your father's wishes for another. You can't just come here and think that you're the law now, Ladybug."

"But isn't that the very reason you asked me to move back, Alma? I'm gonna chalk this up to you being in your feelings because now you *finally* see that dad's mortality is a very real thing. I'm not going back and forth about this either. Daddy, I love you so much. I don't want to lose you over something preventable. I need you to understand that this is all for your greater good. I'm not being a hard ass for no reason. Alma, we gotta be on one accord with this one."

My father let out a long sigh before uttering, "Fine."

His speech was still a bit slurred, but I hoped that his acquiescence finally meant that he was taking his health more seriously than before.

"I'm gonna get out of here, but Alma are you staying overnight? If so, do you need me to bring you back anything?"

She shook her head, face still screwed up because she had been put in her place. Oh well, she'd be alright. I walked over and kissed my dad on the top of his head, leaning over to hug him. "Love you, old man. I'll be back tomorrow, alright? Alma if you get an update about his move to the rehab center just text me, okay?"

"Mmmhmm," she replied.

I looked over at Way who'd been sitting quietly through all the drama. He stood, ready to trail me from the room until my dad spoke up. "H-hold up, b-boy. W-w-we needatalk." All of his words were so mashed together I lowkey wanted to laugh at him trying to call Wayland out, but I didn't say anything.

"Yes sir, " Way replied and then asked Alma to give him and my dad a minute alone before turning toward where I stood, still in the doorway. "Wait for me?"

I nodded and left the room, with Alma not far behind me. Even though I could tell she was still peeved at me, she couldn't resist teasing me. "So you all finally gave up the ghost, huh?"

I smiled immediately. "We're... testing the waters."

"Child, the way that boy puffed up his chest as soon as Kenny said they needed to talk, I'd say y'all already swimming deep off in those waters. Glad he's stepped up. These next few months are about to test us."

I nodded. "But they're necessary, you see that right? I promise I wasn't trying to step on your toes here."

"I know, baby. I just...this is hard for me," she replied.

"Which is why we need to make sure we join forces to get him to act right, not be at odds while trying to placate him."

"I see your point, Ladybug. It's just... easier to let him get his way sometimes. You know how your father is."

"And I know how *you* are. You know he'll follow your lead even if he fusses the whole way there," I said to which Alma laughed.

"You're right, baby. I just don't be wanting to have to hear his mouth all the daggone time."

"But if we let him get his way, we might not hear his mouth at all anymore," I replied soberly.

Her sharp intake of breath let me know the statement had impacted exactly how I'd meant it to. Thankfully, Wayland came through the door right after I'd said that.

"Ready, baby?" he asked and I nodded.

He gave Alma a quick hug and kiss before grabbing my hand and lacing our fingers together as we headed toward the elevator.

"You gonna tell me what that little chat you and Kenny had was about?" I asked as soon as the elevator doors closed.

"Nope," he replied, grinning. "Just a lil man business is all."

"Sounds like some chest pounding bullshit to me."

"If that's how you think it went, then sure. Soooooo... am I following you home or are you trailing me home?"

"And if my answer is neither?"

"I'm not above snatching your ass up and putting you in my truck," he replied easily. "You don't need to be alone right now, so cut the shit."

"Your place it is," I said and he nodded his head.

"Thought you'd see things my way."

Once we got to his place, we settled and ordered out something to eat since my appetite had now come back with a vengeance since I knew that my father wasn't on the verge of leaving us anytime soon. We were ultra-cozy, nestled together on his massive couch while we awaited the food delivery, watching a movie. Tony was sitting up, his back braced against a corner of the sectional, while I laid with my head in his lap, stretched out along one side. His fingers absentmindedly massaged my scalp and I damn near drifted off to sleep from how relaxing the sensation of his movements was.

"Tony?" I said.

"Yeah, baby."

"Thank you."

"For what?" he replied, sounding a little put out so I turned to be able to look up at him.

"Are you serious? For holding me down through all of this mess over the past few—" I started and he cut me off.

"You don't have to thank me for doing what your man should do in this position."

"But we're new and this is a lot and—" I trailed off, looking away, feeling my eyes start to well with tears because I was overwhelmed. As much as I was trying to keep it together, all of this was so fucking much. The hits seemed to be coming in rapid succession and there was nothing I could do to stop them.

"And nothing," he cut in again, shaking his head. He braced a hand beneath my chin, turning my head so our gazes fused once more. "Yes, us exploring the romantic relationship between us is new, but me having your back isn't, baby. You don't ever have to thank me for making sure that you're good. That's the one thing I'm always going to do, past hiccups be damned, aight?"

"Okay," I whispered.

The doorbell rang and he shifted me so he could get up and answer it, essentially ending this conversation that I'd started for...absolutely no reason. Well that was a bit of a lie, I was in my head a little, wondering if all of this emotional heavy lifting was a lot for two people who were just getting their footing back. And I knew I only had qualms about it because everything was clicking on all cylinders without any struggle or strain. Most people would be thankful for that and go along with the flow, but not my over-thinking ass. I was too busy trying to mitigate future disasters instead of living in the now and relishing the lack of friction. But if I knew Tony, I knew he wouldn't let me get too far off into that. He was definitely the glass half full type.

"Bring your overthinking ass on in here and get this pasta, girl," he called out from where he was unloading our food from the bags on his kitchen island. I rolled my eyes, at my own predictability and his uncanny ability to see that shit and call it out plainly. And then got my ass up and got that pasta like he'd told me to.

* * *

"I can't believe I let you talk me into this," I grumbled as Ciji came through my front door on ten.

"You're such a haterrrrrr," she trilled, then giggled. "What's the use in dating brothers if we don't do all the headass shit like double dates and couples game nights? Besides, you could use the diversion. You have been going hard between every-thing with your daddy and the boom in business after MM started airing. Tonight will be the perfect stress relief."

A little over a month had passed since my dad had been transported into the rehab hospital and he was doing really well. Like she'd promised, Alma was making his ass actually put in effort when it came to his rehab and physical therapy. She'd even convinced him to speak with the psychiatrist on staff at the hospital so that he could dissect his feelings about having these physical limitations heaped upon him so suddenly and what it felt like to work through them. According to the doctors at the rehab center, my daddy could be home with us again in as little as another month, something that was a weight off my shoulders. Ciji was right though, I had been working myself to the bone. Thankfully though, Tony had been beside me the whole way, propping me up when I felt like I was about to keel over, sitting me down when I was doing too much. He cared for me and loved on me in a way that was unlike any man

I'd ever been involved with before and it was truly everything.

Tonight we were getting the gang together for a lil game night situation. Even though I kept giving Ciji shit for it because it was her idea, I was lowkey excited to have a night with the crew—talking shit and getting lit. It was something that was well overdue.

"If that is the case then why are we having this little gathering over here and not at your place?" I asked, with a mock scowl.

"Because you've got the fire pit in your backyard and I've got a sex dungeon that I don't want to explain to my coworkers in my basement."

"But like...wouldn't they expect that considering your show?"

"I mean yes, but also...considering I'm dating another person who works with us, I'd rather much let them assume what they think we have going on over them having it confirmed, you know?"

"Mmmmhmmm," I hummed, then giggled.

"Anyway, the guys are picking up the barbecue, this is the last of the desserts I made, and we're good on drinks, right?"

Looking over to my bar cart that was overflowing with bottles thanks to Ciji, I nodded.

"Uh yeah. Girl you dropped off that case like two days ago. I know you didn't think I consumed that much since then?"

"Life has been real *real* for you lately, girl. Wasn't no judgment if you had," Ciji replied, tittering.

"Where in the hell did you get all of this damn liquor anyway?"

"Lovie knows a guy. Who that guy is and how she knows him remains a mystery to me. I don't ask her any questions of which I'm afraid of the answers, so I just thanked her and took the bottles."

I full out laughed then, thinking about her sassy ass grandmother. I'd had occasion to cross paths with her a time or two and she was a hoot. I could only imagine what her "knowing a guy" actually meant.

"I hope you passed along my gratitude then," I replied.

"Of course, boo. Aight, so who you think is gonna get here first?"

"Definitely Rachel. She can't wait to trot her boy toy in here like he's a show pony. She kept mentioning how she couldn't wait for us all to meet him."

"Girl, if she woulda said that shit in the gc one more time, I was about to snap. But, I too remember how I couldn't shut my trap about William when I first put that thang on him, so I'm chillin'."

"You swear you had me sprung from that first night," Will droned as the brothers walked through the door and he and Ciji started going back and forth about who was sprung first.

I shook my head at them as Wayland placed the aluminum pans he was carrying on the stove and walked over to greet me.

"Hey, baby," I crooned, settling into his embrace and tilting my head upward for my kiss.

He pressed his lips to mine briefly with a loud smack, then said, "You ready to make these niggas mad when we win every game tonight?"

"Oh, we're partners? Coz I had told Ciji..."

"I know that's a damn lie. Bruh's too damn possessive to even let his girl have a different partner for five minutes, let alone a whole night. Besides, you're too competitive not to remain paired with the winningest nigga in the building."

"You win one little funky hand of Spades and now you the winningest," Ciji called out.

The doorbell rang and I pulled myself from Tony's grasp to go let whoever in. Opened the door to find Rachel, her new boo, Cienna, Curt, Timi, and his man Branden all on the other side.

"What the hell? Did y'all niggas caravan?" Wayland asked from just behind me and I turned and slapped him on the arm before stepping aside to let everyone in.

After telling them to make themselves at home and pointing out where all of the pertinent things— food, drinks, the restroom—were located, everybody settled in, chowing down before we brought out the games. Pretty quickly it turned into a battle of the sexes, with the women coming out on top even though technically we were at a disadvantage due to the unevenness of the group's sizes. Countless accusations of cheating and home cooking were levied, most notably coming from my sore loser ass boyfriend. After a bit the games gave way to casual conversation, each of us nestled up with our partners on my outdoor patio as a fire blazed in the pit. Gazing around at everyone, I couldn't help but smile at this, something I'd wanted for however long and had denied myself of, a stable community of friends and a loving relationship with a man who was unrepentantly in my corner. I had no idea what moving back home would look for me initially, but now I saw that it was definitely the best move I could have ever made.

Wayland

I couldn't believe that I'd managed to keep this hidden from KK for this long, but today was the day that all of the work me and my team had been putting in, with Alma as my co-conspirator. When he'd initially gone into the rehab hospital the estimation was that he would be there for about sixty days before given the all clear to come home. Unfortunately, the severity of the scope of his rehabilitation had been underestimated so that had come with extended time he needed to spend in the rehab hospital. All of that had been quite harrowing for KK and Miss Alma both, but we'd managed to get through it all by leaning on each other and providing all of the support that Big Kenny had needed by making sure at least one of us, including my dad and brother, made our way to see him daily and kept encouraging and keeping his spirits up.

Since we had finally gotten a "come home" date for Big Kenny, and were facing the likelihood that he would be bound to his wheelchair as he continued to get his strength to walk with the aid of the walker and his cane back, I'd decided to go ahead do some upgrades to the house. I assembled a crew of a few local guys who I tried to throw work toward whenever I had some to spare. Then I finagled my way into the permits by pressing on some officials who owed me favors so that we could get this knocked out fairly quickly. A job that would have normally taken about two to three months we'd managed to get done in just over two months because my guys hopped right in as soon as they could and got busy.

I hadn't been doing as much of the manual labor, mostly just overseeing the changes that their place underwent over the past few weeks, but one of my guys had fallen ill so I'd pitched in over the past couple of days, putting in the elbow grease needed to ensure that everything was done on time before Big Kenny would be home. Alma had done a great job at distracting KK from coming over while renovations were happening, but the text that I'd just gotten from her when I randomly checked in to see what she was up to let me know that my spot was about to be blown up.

I could see this going one of two ways: either she'd be moved by my efforts to surprise her and her pops or she'd be ready to come down on me for spending too much money for something that she hadn't deemed a necessity. Knowing Big Kenny how I knew him, however, I knew that his independence was something that he treasured above most things. So having to be fully reliant upon his wife once he returned home would not be the move. As such, we'd eliminated some of the walls on the first floor, making their floor plan much easier the maneuver through, added a wheelchair lift to make it easier for him to get from the first to the second level easier, and also knocked the wall between Big Kenny and Miss Alma's bedroom and the guest room to expand their master suite and bathroom. What used to be KK's room, would now serve as the guest room going forward.

Today I was outside, building a ramp that ran alongside the house perpendicular to the wrap-around porch so that it would be easier to transport Big Kenny in and out of the house in his wheelchair. KK was supposed to have been at the retail nursery for Worthington Farms today because her manager on duty had an emergency that required her to miss work today, but then the assistant manager had shown up so she said she was pulling up to her folks' house to check in with Alma to make sure they were all set with everything for Big Kenny's homecoming. A quick check of her location showed me that she was too close for me to even try and disguise what we had going on here, so instead I just forged ahead working, knowing that my time of reckoning was coming sooner rather than later.

About ten minutes passed before I turned to see Kalise's car slowly pulling into her folks driveway. I could see the confusion on her face at the guys in the yard through her windshield and when she finally noticed that I was standing among them she got out of the car and headed straight in my direction. I removed the hard hat I was wearing, bracing it under my arm as I clutched the ramp plans in my hand and brought them to rest upon the brightly colored construction vest I wore. With a brilliant grin I hoped would distract her momentarily, I met her halfway.

"What is this?" she said once we were standing in front of one another.

"Just a little project," I replied lightly.

"Ummmmm, anything that requires you to be wearing a hard hat doesn't seem like anything little to me," she retorted.

"Safety first around these parts, baby," I replied as I pulled her into a loose embrace and pressed a kiss to her lips. "And hello to you too, miss rudeness."

She rolled her eyes and shook her head. "Just... what else exactly have you been doing over here? Is this why Alma has been weird every time I try to come over lately?"

Without waiting for me to answer, she took off toward the front steps, making her way through the front door. I was quick on her heels and caught her gasp of surprise, widened eyes, and low utterance of, "Oh my God". I hoped that all of those were good indicators of her astonishment. She whirled around to face me.

"You did all of this?" she asked.

I shook my head. "Not alone. I had some guys come over and hook a few things up for your folks is all. Nothing too major."

"Babe," she said, utter shock dripping from her tone. "This looks like a brand new house." She paused to take everything in. "I was... I was so worried about how my dad was going to maneuver in here and I know you'd mentioned making some modifications, but I knew that they didn't really have the money to be doing all of that and you...why would you do this?" I could see the tears cresting in her eyes and I instantly moved forward to envelop her in my embrace.

"Because I told you that we were in this together. And I meant that shit, Kalise. Plus, I know your pops, he woulda drove Miss Alma insane with the old floor plan. Which, in turn, would have led to her driving you insane as she complained about his stubborn-ness. So, this was a selfish act when you take a look at it for real."

"Shut up," she said, slapping my arm as she leaned up on tiptoe to press a soft kiss against my lips. "Thank you. Because you did not have to do any of this. Hell, I'm not even sure how you managed to pull all of this off. But you did it simply because you knew how much it would mean to me and I..."

"What did I tell you, girl? Stop thanking me for doing shit that is fundamentally basic when it comes to my responsibilities as your man. This shit here was small to a giant, but also a big priority since I'm here to make life easier for you, not let obstacle after obstacle set you back. How many ways do I have to hammer this point into your hard ass head, baby? As long as I'm by your side, you won't have to bear anything burdensome because as soon as I can alleviate it, I'm doing that shit, aight?"

Looking up to me with those unshed tears, she nodded softly before repeating, "Aight."

Afterword

About the Author

Nicole Falls is a contemporary Black romance writer who firmly believes in the power of Black love stories being told. When Nicole isn't writing, she spends her time singing off key to her Spotify playlists and pondering the complexities of life. She currently resides in the suburbs of Chicago.

Also by Nicole Falls

The changeup

The restart

The recovery

Nymphs and trojans Series (collaboration with Alexandra warren)

Shots not taken

Bounce back

Standalone Titles

Sparks Fly

Last First Kiss

sugar butter flour love

All I Want for Christmas

A Natural Transition

Release some tension

The pleasure principle

Run it back

www.ingramcontent.com/pod-product-compliance
Lightning Source LLC
Chambersburg PA
CBHW071327140726
47996CB00005B/1865